Books by S.A. Meade

The Endersley Papers

Lord of Endersley
Darkness at Endersley

Stiff Upper Lip

Biscuits and Bunting

Single Titles

Stolen Summer
Orion Rising
Mourning Jack
A Good Feeling
Tournament of Shadows

Tournament of Shadows

ISBN # 978-1-78651-933-7

©Copyright S.A. Meade 2016

Cover Art by Posh Gosh ©Copyright 2016

Interior text design by Claire Siemaszkiewicz

Pride Publishing

Published in 2016 by Pride Publishing, Newland House, The Point, Weaver Road, Lincoln, LN6 3QN, United Kingdom.

Pride Publishing is a subsidiary of Totally Entwined Group Limited.

Printed in Great Britain by Clays Ltd, St Ives plc
1

TOURNAMENT OF SHADOWS

WITHDRAWN

S.A. MEADE

Dedication

For everyone who's shared this amazing journey with me, offered me advice, wisdom and help and a special thank you to the wonderful ladies at TB including Rebecca, my patient and kind editor and Emmy for the beautiful artwork.

Chapter One

I had more important things to worry about than whether the man who trailed several miles behind me was a coincidental traveler or someone with a far more sinister purpose. My horse was hopping lame and I needed to find somewhere to rest. The prospect of dealing with potential trouble in a country ripe with dangerous possibilities did not appeal to me. I patted the animal's warm neck and kept walking, trying my best to ignore the dust and discomfort of the desert.

A hopeful patch of green glimmered in the distance, distorted by the heat. It was promise enough. I urged the horse on. I cleared my mind of everything but becoming the traveling scholar once more. A harmless fool immersed in research for the sake of it, not a paid fool sent to rescue two other idiots. The May heat left me bad tempered. I just wanted to find a place to rest for a day or two, perhaps lie in wait for my unwanted traveling companion. I knew there was a caravanserai on the road ahead but I didn't want the crowds, the braying camels, persistent hawkers. I just wanted peace and quiet.

I talked to myself in Uzbek. I talked to the horse. His ears twitched at the sound of my voice and he let loose a long, flubbering sigh as he hobbled along beside me. The oasis drew closer, rising out of the scorched earth in a cluster of trees and earthen buildings. The horse quickened his step and I hurried alongside him, desperate for cool, green shade and a place to rest, even if it was just a rug laid out beneath a tree. I needed all the rest I could get in preparation for the impossible task ahead.

* * * *

The furnace wind kicked up dust and dead leaves, hurling them across the road. I was glad to leave the desert behind and reach the refuge of the village. I searched for the closest thing they had to an inn—a small, mud-walled building beneath a canopy of trees. The proprietor, a wizened old man with skin like creased, oiled leather hobbled out into the courtyard and offered me a toothless smile. There were a few cots scattered beneath a wood-shingled awning. One or two were already occupied by weary, dusty travelers sleeping in the shade. I chose the bed at the far end, desiring as much peace and quiet as possible, not wanting to be bothered by conversation or company.

The horse came first. I led him to a stable.

"Your horse has a bad limp, sir."

I bent down and examined the injured leg. "I think it's his foot."

The horse shuddered when I reached for his hoof. It was hot to the touch and a close study of the sole revealed a tell-tale black line, which told me that he had an abscess. "Can I have some warm water?"

"Yes, sir." The innkeeper smiled, nodded then walked away.

I searched my saddle pack for the small bags of things I kept for medicinal purposes including Epsom salts, then pulled the knife from my belt. The innkeeper returned with a basin of water and stood watching when I dug my knife into the animal's hoof. The horse groaned and snorted but remained still as pus streamed from his foot. I dropped Epsom salts into the water, then dunked an unrolled bandage into it. Once the cloth was soaked, I wrapped it carefully around the horse's hoof, all under the watchful eye of my host.

"You are a clever man, sir." His grin was brilliant in the seamed leather of his face.

I straightened my back and patted the horse's warm neck.

6

"No, just one who has learnt to care for his horse." I didn't much care for such close scrutiny and hoped the innkeeper wasn't one of those talkative sorts who need to know the life story of each of his guests.

He stooped to retrieve the basin and flung the water onto the dirt. "I will leave you to rest. I will bring you some food later."

"Thank you." I salaamed, made sure the horse was settled then sought refuge on my bed.

It was cool enough in the shade to be comfortable. I lay down on my bedroll and fell asleep to the warbling of a bird in the dusty trees.

* * * *

The sun slipped beyond the walls of the inn. My host carried a tray across the yard and set it on a small table beside my bed. "It is but a simple meal, sir."

I glanced at the bowl of aromatic stew, the cup of cloudy white rice, the pickles and slab of flatbread. "It is a feast after days of traveler's fare. Thank you."

He left me to eat in peace, which I did, until the bowl was empty, wiped clean by the last wedge of warm bread. I washed the repast down with the lukewarm tea he'd provided. It was more than enough to satisfy me. I returned the tray to the house then went to see to my horse.

The gelding dozed, resting his afflicted foot. I removed the bandage and poultice, pleased to note that the wound had finished draining. There was still some heat in the sole, which meant I faced a day or two of enforced rest.

"It's all right, my friend," I murmured into his ear. "A day or two isn't going to make much of a difference."

I wasn't sure I believed my own words but I needed a sound horse more than I needed the firearm hidden in my saddlebag. The gelding nudged me, then rubbed his head against my shoulder, seeking relief from some hidden itch. I obliged by scratching his cheek and offering up prayers to every god I could think of to speed his recovery.

A bell rang out in the gathering twilight. The innkeeper, muttering something, hurried toward the gate, no doubt to attend to a new arrival. I returned to caring for my horse, making sure he had enough hay and checking the bandage one last time before leaving him to rest once more. The tired shuffle of hooves on mud heralded the approach of another horse. I turned to see it being led into the stall beside mine. I remained still, squatting beside my animal's legs. Sometimes, tired travelers spoke to their horses, told them things they would never say to another.

I was rewarded for my patience by a handful of words in French. My fellow traveler whispered to his horse, telling him that he could rest for a day or two, that they had earned the chance to sleep, eat and be undisturbed. I stayed where I was, listening to the damp swish of the saddle being removed, the brisk strokes of a brush and finally the soft rustle of a horse worrying its hay. Its rider strode away, his footsteps whispering across the dry, packed soil of the courtyard. He called to the innkeeper in nearly flawless Uzbek. A slight stutter in the cadence of his speech betrayed his foreignness to me. But an unschooled ear would not have known a difference.

"Damn." I rose slowly and stroked my horse's warm neck. The oasis was too small a place to remain hidden. I had to hope that my shadow would be too weary to notice me.

I hurried back to my cot, while my pursuer spoke to the innkeeper about food and haggling over a price for his stay. I noted, with a smile, that I had received a better tariff. Back at my cot, I retrieved my battered copy of the Koran from my pack, opened it at a random page and pretended to read, my finger trailing along the ornate script.

The bed beside mine creaked, feet shuffled in the dirt. A tired sigh heralded the arrival of the other, my pursuer. I lost myself in the masquerade and murmured the words beneath my moving finger.

"'Our Lord is Allah,' and then they stand firm, on them

the angels will descend saying, 'Fear not, nor grieve! But receive the glad tidings of Paradise which you have been promised 'We have been your friends in the life of this world and are so in the Hereafter. Therein you shall have all that your soul's desire, and therein you shall have all for which you ask. An entertainment from the Oft-Forgiving, Most Merciful.'"

I turned to the next page and lowered my head, moving my lips, whispering the words.

"*Hayirli kech*" His Uzbek was nearly perfect.

"*Hayirli kech*." I glanced up at the new arrival, keen to see what he looked like, this shadow of mine. It was almost impossible to ignore the sudden quickening of my pulse, the moisture that cooled my palms and stilled my fingers from their wandering across the page.

He was tall, as tall as I was. He traveled under no pretense, dressed in a foreigner's clothes, dusty and worn. There was no possible way he could pass for a local in any event, with auburn hair that caught snatches of fire in the flickering lamplight. He regarded me with stormy gray eyes. A smile of some sort tugged at one corner of his mouth.

I returned the smile, hoping it was the naïve smile of a simple scholar, one who was absorbed by his study of his Koran.

He nodded, then spoke once more. "*Sizning ismingiz nima? Mening ismim* Valentin Yakolev."

"*Mening ismim* Rashid."

He held out his hand in greeting. I reached across and accepted it, resigned to the loss of what little privacy I had. He wrapped his hand around mine, squeezing, proclaiming some kind of dominance. I tried to ignore the sudden blind flutter of my stomach, the kind one experiences when they see someone long absent from their life, that spark of recognition.

I squeezed back and took a stealthy, deep breath, trying to recover from that strange shock. His hand fell away, fingers trailing across my damp palm. Another quirk of the lips. He murmured something I didn't quite catch and sank onto his cot. I took the gesture as one of dismissal and returned to my feigned perusal of the Koran. All the while, everything in me raced and churned and rolled. After a while, his breaths lengthened and slowed. I stole a glance and found him sleeping, hands resting on his stomach, long pale fingers linked together like a simple puzzle. They did not look like the hands of a killer.

I hoped that he wasn't.

Chapter Two

I woke at dawn, before taking my small, worn prayer rug then venturing into the cool shade of the courtyard. I faced Mecca and began the Fajr, the morning prayer. Whether Yakolev saw through my disguise or not, I had to maintain the pretense.

"I offer Fajr prayers, two Rakats, seeking nearness to God, in obedience to Him."

A breeze whispered through the tree, stirring the dappled shade. One of the horses whickered softly.

"Allah is Great."

I hid myself within the comfort of ritual, ignoring the twinge of guilt for saying a prayer I did not believe in. "In the Name of Allah, the most Compassionate, the Merciful."

Small brown birds quarreled beside the somnolent fountain. Morning sunlight crept over the wall and turned the idling droplets of water to silver.

"All praises belong to Allah the Cherisher, the Sustainer, Developer and Perfector of the worlds, the most Compassionate, the Merciful." There was comfort in the recitation, a routine I needed. "Master of the Day of Judgment. Thee only do we Worship, and Thee alone do we ask for help."

A cockerel's raucous call broke the silence. I stole a glance across the courtyard. Yakolev sat on the edge of his bed, shameless in his perusal of my ritual. His hair was mussed, and I clung to the words in an effort to disregard the urge I felt to smooth that hair back, to feel it between my fingers.

"Keep us along the straight path, the path of those whom Thou has blessed." Never truer words. "Not of those whom

Thou art angry, nor of those who go astray."

Still he watched. I finished the first *Surah* and launched into the second. It was a relief to drop onto my knees and prostrate myself, resting shaking hands on the stressed, soft threads of silk. "Glory to God. Free from all defects is my All-Highest Lord, and with His praise I adore Him."

The cockerel called again. Yakolev held a flask in his hands, sipping from it while I sat back on my heels. "I ask Allah, my Lord, to cover up my sins and unto him I turn repentant."

The breeze touched my face, almost like the brush of fingers over skin. I closed my eyes, not wanting to know if I still had an audience. Torn between anger and hope. I had been alone too long. I prostrated myself again. "Glory to Allah. Free from All defects is my All Highest Lord, and with His praise I adore Him."

I'd sought refuge in my work, afraid that remaining close to temptation would drive me insane. I had fought my unholy longing for the touch of another man for far too long. It was better to run from that temptation, to keep my own company. Now, temptation had found me, sat beneath the faded wooden awning of an inn on the Silk Road. I cursed my body while I pretended to pray, I cursed it for wanting a man who had probably been sent to kill me.

By the time I'd finished the morning prayer and rolled up my rug, the innkeeper had brought breakfast, setting it on the small table between the two beds. "You may as well share," he said. "There is plenty here. The bread is fresh and the honey is from a hive just beyond my wall."

The battered brass tray was piled high with soft pillows of flat bread. A floral scent rose from the honey. What made me happier was the tea. The aroma alone was enough to shock me into wakefulness.

My breakfast companion tore off a piece of bread and dunked it into the honey. I followed suit. The honey hinted at cherry blossoms and tasted of spring.

We ate in silence, reducing the precarious tower of bread

to a scant handful. The honey receded in the bowl.

"Are you traveling?" Yakolev asked.

"I am on my way to Bukhara. To the Madrassah."

"You are obviously a devoted man."

I shrugged. "I do my duty to Allah. I wish to learn more." I hoped that he couldn't see through my disguise. Thankful that the O'Riordans were 'black Irish', which made it easier for me to pass as someone called Rashid.

"Your devotion is to be commended." He shared out the last of the tea. "It is a testing journey in this heat. Do you continue your journey today?"

"My horse is lame. I'm waiting for him to recover. The rest will do me no harm." I hoped.

He glanced past me to the stables where both horses dozed in the early morning silence. "Lame?"

"An infection in his foot, nothing more. I have drained the infection and applied a poultice. He will be fine in a day or two." I sipped my tea and wiped honey from the side of the bowl with my last piece of bread. "What about you?" I didn't see why *he* should be the only one to ask questions.

"I am also on my way to Bukhara."

I considered my reply. "Sir, forgive me for being blunt, but the Emir is no mood to see foreigners in his city. Rumor has it that he has two Europeans in his dungeons. I fear if he sees you, he may take you as a third prisoner."

Yakolev set down his tea cup and folded his hands together on one knee. "I doubt that. I come with letters from the Tsar. He will see me."

My heartbeat gained momentum. Almost at once, I wished I could turn tail and head for India. My employers would want to know. "It is said that the two Europeans sought an audience with the Emir and had letters of introduction from their ruler. It is also said that those letters were not enough, that they angered him. I hope that your Tsar has the eloquence to ensure that you are not seen as a threat."

"I have some experience dealing with rulers such as the Emir."

My hackles rose at his arrogance and certainty. It was blind confidence and arrogance that had earned my compatriot, Charles Stoddart, a place in the Emir's dungeons in the first place. "I hope you are right, sir. The Emir is not known for…trusting foreigners, regardless of the promises they may offer."

He drained the last of his tea. "We shall see. I intend to rest for a day or two, then carry on. Perhaps we could travel together."

I stared at him for a moment or two. He stared back. "Do you think riding with me will offer you some kind of protection? Sir, I am a simple scholar of Islam. I have no pull with the Emir or any of his court. Do not assume that being with me will buy you any favors."

"I wish only for companionship. Nothing more. I have been on my own for too long. A little company is all I seek."

I took another sip of tea and studied him, returning his frank appraisal. Had he not been so pleasing to the eye… "All right, but I hope you are not in a hurry. I will not ride to Bukhara until my horse is sound."

"That's fine. I would rather delay my arrival and arrive refreshed than arrive weary and alone."

"I understand. I hope you will not chafe when I pause for prayer."

"Of course not." He offered me a smile. "Your devotion is an example I should learn to follow."

"I am glad you feel I set a worthy example, sir. There is much to be gained in adhering to the teachings of Allah."

"Perhaps you will teach me."

"As you wish." If nothing else, the company would make the journey more interesting. He would be far more pleasing on the eye than the relentless, flat desert.

* * * *

I removed the poultice from my horse's hoof. He stood quietly, idly flicking his tail at flies. His sole was finally cool to the touch, the poultice clear of discharge.

"So we can travel again, my friend." I stood and patted his shoulder.

He turned and nudged me, clearly back to his usual self. Apprehension fluttered in my gut. His lameness had given me a good excuse, now I had no choice but to ride into the lion's jaws…accompanied by a jackal, albeit a handsome one.

I slipped the bridle over the horse's head and led him into the courtyard. Yakolev rested against a post. The evening breeze toyed with his hair and his gaze was keen as he focused on the animal's stride. "He looks sound to me."

"Yes, he is, sir." I turned the horse and watched him, relieved that everything seemed to be fine. "I think we can leave in the morning. I am sure you are anxious to deliver your letters to the Emir."

"I don't know." He stepped into the courtyard. "I am enjoying the rest. I've stayed in worse places than this. The lodgings are a bit…primitive, but the food is splendid."

"The food is very good." I took the horse back to the stable, removed the bridle and gave him some hay.

Yakolev stood in the doorway and watched while I ran a brush over the gelding's flanks. I wasn't sure what he was looking for or at. I hated that his scrutiny left my nerves raw and my instincts tangled.

"You have a very sure hand with that animal." He leaned against the wall. "Like a cavalry man of many years' standing."

"I have been around horses since I was a child." That part wasn't a lie. "My father bred them."

"Yet you chose religious study."

I shrugged, then picked up the horse's long tail and swept the brush through the black strands. "My brother took over when my father became too frail." That also wasn't far from the truth. The younger son never made out well when the spoils were divided. My elder brother took over the running of the estate and I followed the O'Riordan family tradition

15

of joining the 8th Irish Hussars.

Obviously, some things could not be disguised. I set the brush aside, checked the water trough and wiped the dust from my hands. "So I have always worked with horses. I am flattered that you think so highly of my skills, sir."

Yakolev shrugged. "I am a cavalry man myself. I recognize a horseman when I see one. You are a riddle."

"I am a simple man." This conversation needed to end. I closed the stable door and slipped past my inquisitor, afraid of how much more he saw beyond my masquerade.

"You are an interesting man."

"You are the only one who finds me so." I returned to my bed and picked up the prayer rug. "If you'll excuse me, it's nearly time for *isha*."

"Ah, sorry. Far be it from me to interfere with your evening devotion." Yakolev sank onto his cot and folded his arms behind his head while he stared up at the ceiling.

"Thank you. I knew you'd understand." I retreated to the courtyard, spread the rug across the dirt and commenced the final prayer of the day. I soon lost myself in the ritual, forgetting everything, even the man I knew who watched me while I recited the words with as much feeling as an infidel such as myself could muster. By the time I'd finished, the innkeeper had delivered the evening meal. The aroma of stewed mutton and spices drifted across the courtyard, reminding me that I was hungry and it would be the last decent meal I would probably eat until I reached Bukhara.

Yakolev scooped up a mouthful of stew from his bowl with a small funnel of bread. "I'll miss the food here."

"So will I." I didn't want to talk. I just wanted to savor the meal. The fragrant scent of fresh dill drifted from a bowl piled high with tomatoes and green onions. Fragments of the local briny cheese speckled the salad.

We ate in silence. The courtyard was swallowed by darkness. Night birds called out in the trees and the water whispered in the fountain. I hated to admit to myself how much the humble little inn had crawled beneath my skin.

My mission to Bukhara was feeling more and more like a fool's errand and the inn was looking more like paradise.

Yakolev pushed his empty bowl away and plucked a handful of grapes from the bunch draped over the edge of the battered tray. "Have you been to Bukhara before?"

"No."

"Will you be staying at the Madrassah?"

"No."

"An inn?"

"No." I wasn't about to tell him that I had a place to stay with one of our contacts, a rug merchant who was happy to take the Queen's shilling in exchange for providing a safe haven and sending information of import our way.

My companion raised an eyebrow and popped the last grape into his mouth, pushing it to one side so that his cheek bulged. He sucked on it slowly, clearly savoring the sweet and sour juice of the fruit. "So you intend to sleep on the street?"

"I have a place to stay. A friend of the family."

"Ah, I see."

I took some cherries from another bowl. Their garnet skin gleamed in the flickering lamplight and the scent of them rose from my cupped palm. I planned to enjoy each and every one, hopefully without further inquisition from Yakolev. He finished his last grape and reached for the cherries, scooping several up in his hand. He studied them, a frown on his face.

"Is there something unpleasant in the fruit?" I asked.

"No, far from it. They look heavenly. This is why I like traveling these old Silk Roads, such beautiful fruit, such handsome sights. He raised his head, his gaze unwavering. "Don't you think?"

I shrugged. "I have lived in this part of the world all of my life. Perhaps I take such treasures for granted."

He sighed. "For a man of God, you see very little beyond your faith."

"I prefer to look inward." It was easier to hide behind a

cloak of ritual and prayers. "There is much to be found in the words of the Koran and praise of Allah."

"Ah, to find peace so easily. I envy you, Rashid."

"You can find peace in yourself if you wish." I was almost beginning to believe in this persona I'd created.

Yakolev shook his head and popped a cherry into his mouth. "I think I have caused too much trouble in my life to ever find my own tranquility. I have been deplorably spoiled, and very very bad."

Something in his voice, an odd mixture of regret and wickedness tugged at me, tempting me to delve deeper, to find out what he'd left behind. "You are running from something? Someone?"

"Perhaps. If I were to tell you of the life I've led so far, you would surely expect me to burn in hell. I am the darkness to your godly light. My soul, I fear, is beyond saving." He gently extracted the cherry stone from his mouth and placed it into his empty bowl. "The tales I could tell would horrify you."

"I am not easily repulsed, sir. Just because I have tried to lead a blameless life, doesn't mean that I don't know what the 'other side' is like. Perhaps that is why I cling to my God, to redeem myself for misdeeds."

He laughed. "Now you are teasing me. I don't believe for one moment that you have done nothing more sinful than cast a lustful glance at a pretty girl."

Not a girl, never a girl, never a woman.

"It has been a long time. I travel alone and have never taken a wife."

"You are wise, sir. I've never been interested in marriage myself, much to my family's disgust. That is why I choose to travel these roads and do what I do. The farther away I am from St Petersburg, the farther away I am from my mother's accusatory looks and her poorly veiled wishes for grandchildren."

I sipped my cold tea and wished for something a little stronger. I had a flask in my saddlebag. A tot of whiskey would've gone down a treat. "You don't wish to marry, sir?"

"No. No, I do not. I have seen my compatriots strapped to the misery of the obligations of marriage and families. It is not for me, that life."

"So you have run away from it."

"Yes." He spat the last of the stones out. "I prefer my own company. What I really want, I cannot have." His voice was heavy with longing, a child wishing for the impossible.

Something inside me stirred. It wasn't that he was handsome, that his lips begged to be kissed. For a fleeting moment, I wanted to taste the cherry juice on his tongue, to curl my fingers into his hair. Then it passed. But in that moment, I'd recognized what it was that he was running from, that same temptation that I had fled.

Chapter Three

The wind sent eddies of pale dust across the road. My horse snorted and lowered his head, flinching as a dried leaf whirled toward him. Yakolev's horse skittered sideways, spooked at something. He cursed in French, as any well-born Russian gentleman would do, and spurred it on.

I busied myself by staring at the scenery, such that it was. I was in no mood to continue the previous night's conversation. He had strayed perilously close to nudging me toward the truth, as if he knew I was hiding behind my native costume and the beard. When I reached Bukhara, I was determined to trim the bugger. I hated it. For the time being, I had to live with it. I scratched, trying not to let him know that it bothered me beyond endurance, especially in the relentless late spring heat.

"I see a village ahead. I suggest we stop there for the night."

I stared along the track and spied the clump of green trees that heralded a break in the parched landscape. The desert gave way to fields of carefully tended cotton. The horses quickened, sensing water and rest. Another day's journey would bring us to Bukhara. I wasn't sure if I welcomed the end or dreaded it—I would be trading one set of dangers for another. I almost preferred the risk of Yakolev uncovering my deceit than the greater danger of the impossible task ahead of me.

"You are very quiet," my companion observed.

"I have nothing to say."

"No, you don't." He studied me for a long moment. "You even ride like a cavalry man."

"I ride as I was taught."

Yakolev glanced away and chewed his lip. I watched him then turned my attention back to the road. The village rose out of the soil, a low mud wall, blessed shade and a cluster of buildings huddled together. I could only hope that the inn, if there was one, would be half as comfortable as the one we'd left behind.

One more night, that was all. I wanted to shed the disguise, be myself. At least in the merchant's house, I would be able to do just that. The pretense had become a burden, made harder by Yakolev's keen eye.

"What do you think?" Yakolev reined his horse in at the gateway.

I peered past him into the village. It really was little more than a collection of simple houses. Several children chased each other beneath the dappled shade of the trees, while one or two women squatted in the dirt, sorting fruit into bowls. "I see nothing that looks like an inn."

My companion sighed. "Neither do I." He slid from his saddle and ran his hand through his dusty hair.

"Can I help you, sirs?" An elderly man had appeared out of nowhere. "Perhaps you are looking for somewhere to stay?"

"Yes, we are." Yakolev spoke his almost flawless Uzbek. "We are tired, our horses are tired and we need somewhere to rest for the night. Is there anywhere?"

"We have no inn here, but you are welcome to stay with us. I have a farm, there's a place for your horses and you can sleep on the porch, if that is acceptable."

"That would be fine." Yakolev's voice was suddenly weary, as if everything he was running from and toward had caught up with him. "We will pay you handsomely, of course."

"It is no matter, sir. I am always happy to offer a place to rest for weary travelers. Follow me."

I dismounted and followed, along with Yakolev, as our host led us across the dusty village square and along a narrow, shadowed street, which led toward a small field. There were more trees, beneath which sat a slightly bigger house.

"You can turn your horses out here." He nodded toward the little paddock. There is shade and water."

He waited while we unsaddled our animals, then helped us with our belongings. A wrought iron gate opened onto a small courtyard. It was a fraction of the size of the one we had inhabited for the previous few days, but it appeared no less welcoming. A woman, large and comfortable in a silk robe, reclined on a low bed while a younger woman, her daughter perhaps, swept the tiled floor of a long portico.

"You can both sleep out here." Our host indicated the far side of the verandah with a generous sweep of his arm.

"Thank you." I glanced at the cots that sat beneath the roof at the end of the building. "That would be fine."

Yakolev grinned. "It is better than I had reason to expect. It looks very comfortable."

"We take in the occasional traveler, so we're always prepared. Go and settle in. There's water in the well so help yourselves. My daughter, Zamira, will bring you some food a bit later." He tottered across the yard, shouting to the reclining woman.

"We have guests, Feruza, time to cook!"

I dropped my belongings onto the floor beside the cot. Yakolev followed suit, before throwing himself down onto his bed with an extravagant yawn. "I'm looking forward to Bukhara. I need to stay in one place for more than a few days."

"Yes. There's a lot to be said for that." I retrieved my prayer rug. I happily anticipated days uninterrupted by prayers. My contact in Bukhara would not expect that of me, thank Christ. I hurried away from Yakolev's persistent scrutiny and went through the tired motions, aware that he watched every move. It was beginning to annoy me.

When I finished, I returned and dropped the rug to the side of the bed. "What is it about my prayers that you find so fascinating? Must you watch everything I do? My prayers are between me and Allah, they are not for your personal entertainment."

Yakolev raised an eyebrow and held his hands, palm out. "I'm sorry. I just find you fascinating."

Something twisted inside. Cold sweat beaded on my palms. I glared at him to hide that fear of discovery, the worry that something I'd done had given me away. "I can't think why. I am a simple man with nothing to hide. If you behave like this in Bukhara, you will find yourself in trouble, my friend."

"I will be careful."

"You can start now by respecting my privacy." I sank onto the cot and grabbed the Koran.

"You are very prickly."

"You are very rude. I will make allowances for the fact that you are an infidel who doesn't know any better."

The taut canvas of his bed creaked. When Yakolev spoke again, his breath was warm on my cheek. "I think that you aren't what you claim to be."

I inhaled deeply. The scent of dust, horse sweat and *him* filled my nostrils. "What am I?"

"I don't know. You ride like a cavalry man, and there's just a faint inflection in your speech, something that isn't entirely *local*."

I forced myself to return his attention. He was close enough that I saw the day's stubble on his chin. "And what else?"

"Your beard." He tugged at it lightly. "You hate it. You're always scratching at it, tugging at it as if you want it gone."

"It's just habit. I've always done that."

"I don't believe you." Yakolev sat back.

A door on the other side of the house creaked open. I glanced up in time to see our host's daughter approaching us, carrying a round brass tray piled high with food. "Kindly refrain from indulging in your ridiculous speculations while we eat. I'd prefer to eat in peace."

23

He held his hands out again in that palm-up gesture. "All right, all right. I will leave you alone. But don't think that I'm done with this."

"Obviously not."

Zamira set the tray on the low table between the beds, smiled and departed, blushing prettily. For a minute or two I almost regretted that women didn't hold much appeal for me.

"This looks splendid, don't you think?" Yakolev picked up a small bowl of rice and spooned a few morsels of stew onto it.

"It does." I took my own bowl and helped myself to some of the meat.

We ate in silence while dusk settled into the courtyard. The village beyond the mud wall fell into silence. A raggedy flock of chickens scratched idly at the dirt while lamps flickered on inside the house. The evening breeze rustled the leaves of a tired lemon tree in the corner of the yard. The fruits glowed in the soft, violet dusk. Had it not been for the presence of my traveling companion who doggedly tucked into his supper, I may have almost enjoyed myself. Instead, I finished my rice and took a piece of warm bread, dipping it into the rich, spicy stew.

"Nice evening." Yakolev set his bowl aside and sat back, crossing his legs, clearly comfortable with himself and his surroundings.

"Yes."

"I sometimes wish I could settle down in a place as tranquil as this. Perhaps I shall."

I thought of what waited for me back in Ireland. Perhaps a cottage on my brother's estate. There were worse fates. The land ran all the way to the coast. I had my eye on a small place just above the beach. It was small, probably damp, but it would be a place to rest and recover after my travels. "Did you have somewhere in mind?"

"My family have a *dacha* north of St Petersburg. It's not a big place and the village nearby is small. But it's quiet and stands in the middle of the forest. It's beautiful in the summer, the evening goes on forever. In midsummer, the sun hardly sets. The forest is full of soft light. I love to lie on the grass and listen to the birdsong." Yakolev paused, his eyes distant, his mind clearly wandering through his forest. "It's even better in the winter. So much snow. No need to see anyone, go anywhere. I can just sit beside the fire with a good book and enjoy my own company."

It did sound nice. I found myself wondering what it would be like. I *saw* myself sitting beside that fireplace, perhaps watching him read, seeing how the firelight glanced off his hair, warmed his skin. My body reacted with embarrassing longing for someone I could never have. The man was dangerous enough. I did not need that distraction, that desire. It was one that could never be satisfied. I reached for a piece of fruit, hoping that the sweetness of it would pull my mind away from that place, that refuge from the heat and dust and futility of my mission.

"What of you? Do you have such a place?"

I shrugged. "No, I have nothing like that. A room in my father's house. It isn't a bad place and I want for nothing."

He lifted an eyebrow and gave me a half smile. "Apart from solitude. Is that why you are always praying? Because that's the only time you can truly ever find your peace?"

"Perhaps it is."

Yakolev plucked a grape from the fruit bowl. "I'll take my *dacha*. I wish I was there now."

I almost wished I was there too.

* * * *

The walls of Bukhara appeared in the flat landscape. The road had ceased to be quiet as we neared the city in the heat of mid-afternoon. The cotton fields spread in a dusty green blanket around the city, giving an illusion of fecundity. Yakolev was silent while he surveyed our surroundings. He'd scarcely said a word since we'd left the village, which suited me just fine. I made a point to leave my beard alone. There was little I could do about the way I rode, I'd known no other way. He could think what he bloody well liked. I would soon be shot of him, once we reached the city gates.

I patted my horse's neck and looked forward to a day or two's hospitality in a friendly, safe house. The first thing I planned to do was to rid myself of that damnable beard.

"So the end of our journey draws near." Yakolev reined his horse to one side to avoid an obstreperous, bawling camel. "I for one will be glad of the rest."

"I'm sure you will." I glanced at him. "Have a care with the Emir, sir. He is in a dangerous mood most days, from what I hear. I have urged you to caution before, and I will do so again. He is not well disposed toward foreigners, regardless of their country of origin."

He shrugged. "I will heed your words. I'll make sure that I approach the palace on foot and that I am suitably humbled in his presence."

"The less time you can spend in his presence, the better." I didn't want to see him harmed. It would be such a…waste. Part of me didn't want to say goodbye, that part that liked watching him shave in the morning, stripped to the waist to reveal a lean, golden brown torso with just a faint and tempting dusting of dark brown hair.

I tightened my fingers around the reins in an attempt to stop the tingling in their tips, the mad desire to brush them over that expanse of skin, to follow that thin line that slipped beneath his navel to the waistband of his breeches.

God save me.

"I do believe you're concerned for my wellbeing." He laughed, reached over and play-punched my arm.

"I am concerned for any man's wellbeing in the presence of such a dangerous, unpredictable man." The punch had felt like a benediction, half a caress, something I wanted more of, more of his touch, damn him.

The walls loomed above us, chalky gray, concealing the maze of shadowed streets beyond. Relief battled with regret and apprehension. Soon enough I would be on my own, free from his ceaseless scrutiny and pointed comments. I was a fool who'd been denied the comfort of another man for far too long. He led the way through the gate and wisely dismounted. If the Emir was out and about, he would not take too kindly to a foreigner boldly riding toward the palace when he should've been on foot. That had been Stoddart's big mistake.

I slid from my horse's back and pulled the reins over his head. "This is where we part company, sir."

Yakolev held out his hand and I took it, not sure whose grip was tighter.

"It has been a pleasure traveling with you, Rashid. Thank you for your company." He shook my hand vigorously, covering it with his other before pulling away. He trailed his fingers along the underside of my wrist.

I bit my lip. "It has been a pleasure traveling with you too, sir."

"Really? I would've thought you'd be glad to be free of my questions."

I couldn't help but smile. "True, sir. I am glad to be free of those. I wish you well. Allah be with you."

"And with you." He backed away. I could not read his face, the mask had slipped into place. "Take care."

"And you." I turned toward the Madrassah, knowing that he would watch me go, that he would make sure.

My horse nudged me as we walked along the busy lane. I didn't look back. I didn't have to. I know he took note of every step I took before I was swallowed by the crowd.

After a little while, I glanced back. There was no sign of him. I steered the horse away from the Madrassah and headed toward the merchant's house and safety.

* * * *

Akmal sank onto his day bed and gestured toward the low table where a feast waited. When I had arrived, he had

27

set his wife and daughters to work in the kitchen while I was shown my room upstairs at the top of the house. After days of sleeping on porches, or out in the open, it was a novelty to find a private place, clean and quiet.

"It is good to see you again, my friend. I hope this humble meal will do."

I stared at the vast array of bowls and platters, there were stews, bowls of rice, vegetables, cheese, a pile of still warm flat bread, fruit, cakes. "It is a splendid feast. Thank you for the honor and the hospitality."

Akmal reached for a slab of bread. "It is the least we could do for you. I have missed our chats."

"How are you finding it here, after Kabul?"

"Peaceful and safe. I like it very much. My family are very happy here, we are prospering and doing well. I have even found a fine husband for my eldest daughter. I will be forever in your debt for your help in settling us here."

"I owe you my life. If you hadn't…"

If Akmal hadn't warned me that trouble was afoot, I would've perished with my countrymen, knee deep in snow, in a mountain pass.

"It was nothing. We owe you *our* lives. We have a good life here."

"I'm pleased to hear it." I scattered crumbs of white cheese onto a piece of bread.

"How was your journey? Did you have any trouble?" Akmal took a sip from his cup.

"I had some unwanted company for the last few days. A Russian."

He stared at me for a moment, his eyes wide. "A Russian?"

"He is paying a visit to the Emir. He comes with a letter of introduction from the Tsar."

"Then he is a blind fool. I think our friend the Emir has had more than enough of foreign emissaries."

"I tried to tell him that but he would not be swayed."

"Did he suspect what…who you are?"

I drank a couple of mouthfuls of wine. "He suspected

something and he was very open about it. He thought I rode like a cavalry man and hated my beard. Of course he was right on both counts, but I could hardly confess, could I?" I rubbed my chin, now freed of its beard. "I suspect he is very familiar with how things are played in this part of the world. He seemed very comfortable in his own skin and more than a little cocky."

"He didn't follow you, did he?"

"No, I was very circumspect. I headed for the Madrassah first, I went as far as the gate. When I looked back and waited, he was nowhere to be seen. I expect he was anxious to find lodgings and prepare for his audience."

"He is a fool. He'll be lucky to escape without being thrown into the Pit with the others."

The blood drained from my face. "Is that where they are? I thought they were under house arrest?" I had no chance in freeing Stoddart and Connolly if they were in the dungeon below the vast fortress.

Akmal patted my arm. "Don't worry, my friend, they are still under house arrest. They should stay there unless the Emir decides he's had enough of them."

I puffed air out of my cheeks. "That's something, I suppose. Where are they?"

"In the Ark. It won't be easy to get to them. I have made a friend of one of the guards. He is our only hope. He is trying to figure out a way to get you in so that you can try to get them out." He shook his head and helped himself to a handful of *plov*. "It will not be easy, not at all."

"Bugger."

"It is, how you British say, a 'forlorn hope'?"

A forlorn hope was every soldier's nightmare. A battle that could not be won. "I'd always thought I was being sent on a fool's errand. I tried to tell them but they wouldn't listen."

"Try not to worry about it for now. It is best that you rest for a few days. I will see what I can find out. There's no point in trying to get you in there, if they've been thrown back in the dungeon."

"I suppose not." The prospect of resting held great appeal, to sleep in a real bed, with a proper roof over my head before sticking my head over the proverbial parapet.

"Now tell me about this Russian."

I thought of Yakolev, and the image that came to mind was of him reclining on the bed in the inn, sleeping in the vague chill of early morning, one arm thrown behind his head while he was lost in dreams. "He was nosey. I am sure that his true purpose in seeing the Emir is less than honorable. No doubt he also brings promises of riches and Russia's support in keeping the British out of his kingdom."

"I hope for his sake that the Emir is in a good frame of mind. One never knows these days." Akmal helped himself to a tomato. "I cannot help but feel that you have been sent into the lion's den, my friend. You must be very careful."

"I intend to be."

"He will be trying to take advantage of what happened in Kabul, point out how weak the British are now. The Russians will be circling like vultures."

"There's still some who think that the Russians had their hand in what happened there."

Akmal shrugged. "It is always possible." He pushed a bowl of stewed mutton toward me. "But let's not worry about that now. Go on, eat. We will worry tomorrow. Tonight is for good food and idle chatter."

* * * *

I wound my way through the bazaar, taking my time, enjoying the novelty of examining the goods on offer. The heat was far more tolerable without the holy man's beard. The native costume also helped. Akmal's reassurance that I would pass through the streets unnoticed as I once had in Kabul proved right. I lost myself in the crowd and caught snatches of conversation – a man haggling with a stallholder over the price of a lantern, an elderly gentleman berating a young boy for running between the stalls, someone wondering aloud where the rug seller was, another asking for directions to the jewelers' bazaar. I paused at a stand selling sweetmeats and nuts, my mouth watering for a treat of some description.

The drift of a scent, a familiar rhythm of footsteps... I didn't need to hear his voice to know he was close by. But there it was, that subtle inflection that wasn't local.

"How fresh are these?" Yakolev asked the man who sold vegetables on the stall next to mine.

I glanced to the side, watching him, pretending to be fascinated by the pile of grapes before me, hoping that he wouldn't recognize me.

"They are very fresh, sir. My wife picked them this morning." Indignation colored the stall keeper's words.

Yakolev chuckled. "Very well, I'll take a couple."

"Thank you."

I froze while he paid the vendor, waiting for him to move on. Instead, he moved closer, obviously wishing to inspect the fruits. I turned away and walked toward the exit, trying not to hurry, trying to look as if I belonged there. After a few moments I paused at another stall and glanced back. He'd been swallowed by the crowds somewhere between the fruit and the rug seller's stall, where I stood. I paused a moment, then headed back, watching carefully. I needed to know where he was staying, so I could steer clear of the place.

His height made him easy to spot above a sea of bobbing dark heads, his foreign clothes made him a mark for every hawker out there. Yakolev strode through the crowd as if he owned the place, as if he expected people to step back in his wake. Some paused and glanced back at him, the tall, pale man with hair that caught light in the morning sunshine. He was easy to follow. I fell into step several yards behind him, always keeping an eye out for somewhere to duck into, should he turn and look back. He didn't. He kept walking, whistling as he did, clear where he was going. I envied his confidence. For a moment, I wanted him and didn't know why.

The streets became quieter, lost in shadow, buildings close together offering shady respite from the desert sun. I slowed, afraid that I would be too easy to spot if he turned around. There were so few people, children running about, squealing, a man chasing a chicken down a dusty alley. Finally, Yakolev paused before a small house with a blue door. He glanced up and down the street then entered, disappearing into the building. I leaned against a wall and caught my breath. It was just a simple house. There would be a courtyard beyond that door, perhaps with a small fountain. More importantly, it was at the opposite end of the city from where I was staying. It was highly unlikely that he would ever find me. I inhaled and exhaled in relief, then headed back the way I came.

* * * *

Akmal sat cross-legged on the day bed and sipped his tea. "It is not good news, I'm afraid."

"Have they been thrown into the Pit again?"

"No, not yet, but my contact seems to think it won't be long. The Emir has doubled the guard around the house. He's cut their rations. Something has angered him."

Something curdled in the pit of my stomach. The fool's errand was descending into the forlorn hope Akmal had mentioned. "Is there any way to get them out?"

"To get them out, you have to get in. You've seen the walls of the Ark. It was built to keep entire armies out. I have my friend looking at some way to get you in. But you will have a dozen guards to subdue before you can even get into where they're being kept. I'm afraid that your friends in Calcutta have sent you here for no reason. It would take a miracle to save your countrymen now."

I wished Akmal had something stronger to hand than

the ubiquitous green tea. Instead, I grabbed a handful of grapes from a beaten brass bowl and stared at them for a few moments. "Have you had any word on my Russian friend?"

"Nothing. Why?"

"I just wondered if he'd found favor with the Emir. I've just had a ridiculous idea, but at this stage in the game, it might be worth a try."

"You've had ridiculous ideas before, my friend. And they've worked."

"I told you I found where Yakolev is staying. Perhaps I should pay him a visit. If he's in the Emir's good books, perhaps I could strike a deal with him, persuade him to put in a good word for Stoddart and Connolly. Perhaps he could persuade the Emir to set them free."

Akmal laughed. "You are clutching at straws. Don't forget, you would be a stranger to him. He traveled here with a pious man, not a British spy. What will you do, grow that beard back and then pay him a visit? If you go down that road, you will have to be truthful with him. If you are truthful, doesn't it undermine everything your government wants? Don't you think they might be a little angry to find you have been doing deals with the Russians behind their backs?"

"Trust you to find the flaws." I tried to smile. "It's clearly impossible, without raising an army, to rescue Stoddart and Connolly. I can't rescue them on my own and I can't risk anyone else's life by seeking help. I'm just clutching at straws."

"What could you possibly offer the Russian?" Akmal took some grapes.

I thought of the way Yakolev had watched me, remembered the veiled references to his less than perfect past, to the hints he'd dropped that he was running from something, the suspicion that he fled the same thing I did — the temptation to sleep with other men.

There *was* something I could offer Yakolev.

My body.

34

Chapter Four

I sat outside the tea house, nursing my cup of tea while I watched life in the bazaar. I watched and waited. After a couple of days, I'd learnt that Yakolev visited the same stalls. He bought tomatoes from the vegetable stall and cherries from the fruit stall, before heading back to his lodgings. According to Akmal, he had yet to succeed in getting an audience with the Emir. He'd be bored and frustrated. I knew how *that* felt. I needed him to be in that frame of mind. The Emir's instability would allow me to play Yakolev right into my hands.

"You're mad." Akmal had said. "It is one thing sleeping with men for pleasure, but doing this…"

"Believe me, my friend, it will not be much of a sacrifice."

He'd shaken his head. "You are a fool."

"Who's been sent on a fool's errand. I think that qualifies me to try whatever measure I can to get the job done."

"Be careful."

"I will be. I promise."

I'd told Akmal where the house was, just to be on the safe side. I'd make sure to leave a trail for him if something were to go wrong.

I sipped my tea then saw sunlight glancing off auburn hair, turning it to a rich, autumnal bay. My pulse quickened. I unfolded my legs and stood up. Not taking my gaze off him, watching while he stood at the vegetable stall and perused the tomatoes. Would he recognize me? Now was the time to find out. With more confidence than I felt, I strode toward the stall, trying to find that arrogance that he possessed, trying to walk with the air of a man who had something good to offer, not someone who had everything to lose.

The fruit seller already knew me. He knew I liked the grapes and had already grabbed a large bunch when he saw me approach.

"Good morning, sir. I have some very nice grapes for you today."

"Thank you, I wouldn't mind some of those cherries while you're at it." I made sure that I spoke loud enough for Yakolev to hear me.

"Certainly, sir." The proprietor scooped up a handful of cherries "They are very fine cherries."

"I can vouch for that." Yakolev's voice was full of humor. "When you're finished with this gentleman, I shall take some of those cherries."

"Of course, sir."

I dared to glance at Yakolev, wondering whether I'd see recognition in his eyes. "I appreciate your endorsement, sir. I hope they are as good as they look."

He grinned broadly. "You sound very familiar to me. Have me met?"

"Yes we have." I moved my hand to where my beard once rested and tugged at the ghost of it.

Yakolev laughed. "Good heavens! It's my holy man. Rashid?"

"In a manner of speaking...yes."

"Now I am full of questions."

I absently paid for the fruit the stall keeper handed me. "I'm sure you are."

He waited for his fruit. "You have some explaining to do."

"I owe you no explanations, sir. I merely found Rashid... convenient."

Yakolev raised an eyebrow. "Obviously. Perhaps you would join me for some tea. We can talk."

"I'd like that."

We walked back toward the tea house, leaving the bustle of the bazaar behind. My mind reeled with possibilities while I tried to spin the right words together, wondering how I could lead the conversation in the direction I needed it to go in. Yakolev found somewhere to sit and gestured to the space beside him before signaling to the proprietor.

"So, I was right, you hated the beard."

"Loathed it."

"I must say, you look far better without it. Less pious."

"Good. Because I'm not a pious man. Far from it."

"I thought as much." He paused when someone brought our tea and set it before us. Yakolev plucked a cherry from his bag and placed it carefully on his tongue. After a moment, he tugged at the stem, chewed then removed the stone. He placed it neatly on the tray. "Why the disguise? Wait, never mind. The way you sit on a horse...I was right, was I not?"

"8th Irish Hussars and a childhood riding horses."

"And you're not here to discuss the Koran with an Imam, are you?"

"No."

He poured the tea then handed me a cup.

"You're here because of those two Englishmen."

"Yes."

"You were sent to try and get them out?"

"Yes."

"Oh dear. It seems you've been given an impossible task, my friend."

"I have. There seems little hope of success."

"Indeed." He set his cup down and leaned back, resting his weight on both hands on the low, cloth-covered bench. "I compliment you on your acting skills. You nearly had me fooled. Well, fooled enough that I found it too risky to attempt to winkle the truth out of you."

"I'm glad it worked. It took a long time to perfect the role."

"For all the good it's done you. Which is to say, none at all." The look in his gray eyes crept fairly close to pity. "So why make yourself known to me now? Surely you're not expecting me to help?"

I took a deep breath, puffed out my cheeks and exhaled slowly. "I did wonder."

"Why would I want to help you? Why should I risk my life? You deceived me. Oh, don't worry, I don't take it personally. You're just doing your job, serving your masters as I must serve mine. I can't help you. It would take more than two of us to free your compatriots. It would take an army and, last time I heard, your army had been soundly whipped in Afghanistan."

"No need to rub it in." I imitated his posture, leaning back, making sure I placed my hand close to his, close enough that I felt the warmth of it.

"So, assuming I agreed to put your deception behind me, what would you want me to do?"

"Have you had your audience with the Emir yet?" I knew the answer to be 'no' but I wanted him to admit it, to see that arrogance deflated a little.

"No. But I assume you already know that." The humor fled from his voice. His eyes darkened to the color of storm clouds. "It seems the Emir is having one of his bad tempered turns. If I were you, I'd be very worried about your friends. You know what the Emir is like when he's in a mood." He nodded in the direction of the tower, which rose beyond the bazaar. "Your friends could be taking a flight from atop that minaret."

"I'd rather they didn't."

Yakolev sat forward, but not before brushing my hand with his. "What did you have in mind? Wait…before this conversation continues, perhaps you could show me the courtesy of giving me your real name, since you're clearly *not* Rashid the pious horseman."

"It's Gabriel, Captain Gabriel O'Riordan."

He extended his hand toward me and shook mine. "It's a pleasure to meet you, sir. It's not often that we get to meet each other in this tournament of shadows. Well, not without bloodshed. I'm hoping this won't end with that. I rather like you, in spite of your lies."

"I rather like you too."

Yakolev took a mouthful of tea. "Now you're just saying that to get round me."

"No, for once I'm telling the truth."

He studied me for a long moment. "Yes, I believe you are. So what do you want from me?"

I stared at my hands, at my cup of tea, at the pattern on the rug that covered the low bench we sat on. "This is…difficult. I hate to fail. That is why I'm scrambling for a solution. I don't know if you can help but I have to try everything." I forced myself to look at him. "When you get your audience with the Emir, perhaps you could ask if they could be freed. Or suggest it. It would show that you represent a country that is magnanimous, even in the treatment of its rivals."

"Or a country too weak to represent itself rather than the interests of others." Yakolev snarled. "You must think me mad. I'd be thrown into the dungeon with them. No, I'm sorry O'Riordan, I won't do that."

I set my cup down and wrapped my arms around my knees. "It was worth a try, I suppose."

"Look, I'm sorry. Just tell me one thing, what the hell did you do to anger your masters?"

I glared at him. "What do you mean?"

"I mean, what did you do that would drive them to send you on a mission that had no hope of success?"

"They didn't believe me when I told them there'd be trouble in Kabul. I knew. I had a very good network of informants. My superior officer wasn't happy about that. I am a junior agent, I wasn't supposed to be *that* good. They sent me to India, told me I was scaremongering. In doing that, they saved my life."

"Only to throw you to the wolves. Our masters don't like being told that they're wrong. It deflates their egos."

"So it would seem."

The sympathy in his voice gave me some hope. I risked a glance and found him smiling, after a fashion. It was a smile laced with compassion and a little pity. "I am sorry. It seems we are in the same boat. I can't say I'm looking forward to my audience with the Emir." He rested back on his elbows and was silent for a few moments.

I picked up my tea once more and stared into the empty cup.

"If I did mention the plight of your compatriots to the Emir, should I find him in a benevolent frame of mind, what would my...reward be?" Yakolev raked me with his gaze. "I don't need money and I suspect your government wouldn't be too happy if you were to spend their gold on me in any event."

"Probably not. But money wasn't what I had in mind." I curled my fingers into my clammy palms.

He tipped his head to one side and offered me a twitch of his lips. "What *did* you have in mind?"

I drew a deep breath and forced myself to look him in the eye. "I think you're running from the same thing I'm running from. Something you said about disappointing your mother, not providing her with grandchildren..."

"Go on." Again, that tiny quirk of the lips.

I dug deeper. "You don't like women any more than I do."

A bird sang out in the sudden heavy silence. I watched Yakolev's face carefully, waiting. His expression was veiled in shadow from the spindly tree in the tiny courtyard of the tea house. His chest rose and fell. He turned onto his side and faced me. "Am I that easy to read?"

"Only to one who knows, who feels the same."

"You *are* full of surprises."

"I am right, aren't I?"

He sighed. "Yes. You are very perceptive. I suppose it comes with the profession. So you think if you offered me your body, I would agree to your request?"

"I had to try." I returned his stare with as much defiance as I could muster. "I saw how you watched me. It struck me as more than curiosity."

40

"You really don't miss much." Yakolev walked his fingers across the bench toward mine. "In spite of your piety, I found something very desirable in you. It made it hard to sleep at night. I kept wondering about what you would look like without the damnable native robes."

"These 'damnable native robes' are very comfortable in this heat."

"I'd rather see you without."

Something inside lifted. "Does that mean...?"

"What it means is that I need to think about it. I need to weigh my desire against the price I may pay for carrying out your request. Do I risk my life for the pleasure I could take from you? Would you be worth it?"

"I'm no virgin, if that's what you mean. I've been told that I'm very good."

He leaned close, as close as decency allowed in such a public place. "I'll be the judge of that."

"I don't think you'd be disappointed."

"Leave me time to think." He stood with a swiftness that took me by surprise. "Meet me here tomorrow and I'll give you my decision."

He disappeared into the bazaar before I could summon a reply.

* * * *

"You are insane." Akmal helped me into my outer robe. "He could kill you."

"To what end? My death would serve no one."

"You hope." He shook his head. "I have turned a blind eye to your...preferences in the past because you are usually clever enough to keep out of trouble. This smacks of desperation and Yakolev knows it."

"Perhaps. We shall see. He will more than likely turn down my offer."

"I hope he does...for your sake."

"I hope he doesn't. I'll see you later." I fled out onto the

41

street and hurried toward the bazaar.

* * * *

Yakolev sat on the same bench we'd shared the day before. He rose when I approached. He'd finally surrendered to the desert heat and had donned native clothing. My pulse raced and I paused in my progress to catch my breath.

"Will you walk with me?" he asked.

I managed a nod and fell into step beside him as he pushed through the crowds.

After a few moments, we found ourselves on a quiet street. Yakolev glanced over his shoulder, then steered me into a narrow, shadowed passageway.

"What—?"

"Hush. Don't worry, I'm not going to murder you." He backed me to the wall. "I just want to sample the wares before I make my final decision."

Before I could speak, he curled his fingers into my hair and pressed his lips to mine, devouring me with a hungry kiss.

I could do nothing but respond, winding my arms around his waist and pulling him closer. His arousal was evident, matching mine. Never before had I responded so readily to a man's touch. Never had I been so desperate for it.

A rooster's late call broke us apart. Yakolev stepped back, chest rising and falling like bellows. He reached out and brushed the hair from my forehead with a tender hand, then grinned.

My lips felt bruised and swollen. "Well?"

"You have my word. When I see the Emir tomorrow, I will suggest that to save him the burden of having two Englishmen and the danger that their countrymen could send an army to free them, I will take them and place them in a Russian gaol because the British would never attack us. It's the best I could come up with. Of course, if he accedes to the request, I will deliver them to you at a pre-arranged meeting point, far away from here. Will that suit?"

I wanted him to kiss me. "Yes. It's a very reasonable plan."

"I'm glad you think so." He brushed his lips over mine. "Assuming he doesn't throw me in the dungeon, meet me at the tea house tomorrow night, so I can collect my payment."

I was grateful that the robe hid my obvious desire. "Yes. I can do that. Thank you."

"No, thank *you*. The thought of what I can do to you will get me through a very difficult appointment. I will just think of how much I want you, how much I have to look forward to."

"Then let's hope the Emir is in a good humor." I ran my forefinger in a straight line from his throat to his groin, earning a fevered gasp for my sins.

Yakolev caught my hand and raised it to his cheek, before turning to kiss my palm. "I'll make sure that he is and I'll make sure that I leave that place in one piece."

"See that you do."

He released me with a sigh. "I'll see you tomorrow."

"Yes."

We slipped out of the passageway and onto the quiet street. Yakolev raised a hand in farewell. "I'll see you tomorrow evening at dusk. You'd best get as much rest as you can." He winked, turned then walked away. I took a deep breath and headed in the opposite direction, wondering how I could get rid of my erection before I returned to Akmal's house.

* * * *

I reached the tea house at sunset as the call to prayer sang out from a nearby minaret. The bazaar was deserted and only a few customers sat on the low, flat benches in the evening shade. Yakolev was not among them.

The proprietor brought tea. I poured myself a cup and settled onto the bench. There wasn't much to observe, apart from the lazy, erratic sway of leaves on the spindly tree in the sullen breeze. A bird sang from a rooftop while people talked in low murmurs all around me. The tea did nothing to calm my racing pulse, or quell the tremor in my hand when I raised the cup to my lips. I watched the narrow street, staring in the direction that we'd headed in the day before.

I drank another cup of tea and watched the light fade from the courtyard. A host of scenarios played themselves out in my mind. Perhaps he had changed his mind and decided not to ask Emir. Perhaps he *had* asked and had been thrown in the dungeon for his cheek. Maybe the Emir had decided to hold a feast in his honor. I just had no way of knowing. I decided to wait until I'd emptied the tea pot before leaving. I had to give him a chance.

"Ah, there you are." He'd crept out of nowhere and sank onto the bench beside me, looking completely at ease in his native clothes. "I suppose you were wondering whether I would make it or not."

"It had crossed my mind." Desire swept through me like the tide.

Yakolev leaned close and whispered, "I would've crawled out of the Pit to collect this reward."

Jesus.

I inhaled deeply and gave up wrestling with my longing. I wanted to grab him by the hand and hurry him to bed. "I'm flattered."

"You should be." He withdrew, leaving his warm breath on my skin as a promise. "The Emir was *not* pleased. I thought for one horrible moment that I'd be imprisoned."

"So he refused."

"He did. I'm sorry. He told me that he is no longer afraid that your countrymen will march on Bukhara, since they were so soundly thrashed at Kabul. I'm afraid your compatriots' days may be numbered."

My stomach turned to lead and sank. "I suppose it was all too much to hope for."

44

"You cannot be held to blame. You were never going to win against a madman such as Nasrullah." He released a sigh. He edged his hand toward mine and brushed his fingers over my skin. "I don't think any foreigner is safe here. As soon as my business is done, I intend to get away as quickly as I can. I suggest you cut your losses and do the same. The British are most definitely not in favor with the Emir right now."

"Thank you for that comforting advice."

"Come, finish your tea. I think we can find a much better way to pass the night, don't you?"

I set the empty cup down and stood when he did. "Yes." I tried to imagine what the night would hold. What kind of lover would he be? It had been so long since I had lain with a man.

The street beyond the bazaar was quiet. A fitful moon lit our way. We walked close enough together that our shoulders touched. The desert night brought a cool breeze. I welcomed Yakolev's warmth and the promise it held. Now and then, his fingers brushed mine.

"Here we are." He paused before the blue door he'd walked through a few days before. "All very small, but private."

I followed him into a tiny courtyard. "I thought you'd stay at an inn."

"This is…some place that is available to certain people. Somewhere for the likes of me to stay." He offered no more information. Instead, he seized my hand and led me toward another door.

I told myself that I was in his debt and I had to do what he wanted. It wasn't normally how matters of the bedroom went, as far as I was concerned, but just this once, my desperation for the touch of another man clouded my thoughts, weakened my will.

"Up here." Yakolev hurried up a narrow, dark staircase, pulling me behind him. He stumbled into a room at the top of the stairs. I nearly tripped over the bed in my haste to follow. The room was washed in shadow, night had fallen with a swiftness not known back home. Yakolev cursed while he fumbled for a lamp, a sudden flare of flame, then the room was filled with a flickering amber light.

"Come here," he whispered. His eyes were as dark and wild as a summer storm. He tore at his robes, pushing them over his head and tossing them carelessly onto the floor. Then he grabbed mine, wrenching them off with some assistance from me, until we both stood naked and breathless.

"Jesus." Yakolev exhaled softly. "You are every bit as beautiful as I imagined you'd be. "I don't even know where to start."

I struggled to breathe, mesmerized. "Do what you will."

He reached out then ran his hand in a wavering line from my throat to my navel. My member leaped at his unexpectedly tentative touch. I did the same to him, and wrapped my fingers around his cock, before dropping to my knees.

"Ah, please. Dear God, Gabriel, please…"

I took him into my mouth, carefully at first, licking my way around the tip, tasting the beads of fluid, which warmed my tongue. The scent of him aroused me, surrounded me.

Yakolev grasped my hair, tightening his fingers and sighing as I set to work. I took as much of him in as I dared, afraid to choke, afraid to falter when I'd already found a rhythm. He groaned and thrust his hips toward me. I cupped one hand around his sac, tickling it, caressing it, driving him closer to relief. Mine could wait.

He spread his legs and braced himself against the wall. His breaths escaped in a staccato of gasps, punctuated by moans. I paused, trailing my tongue along his length, teasing, twirling around the glistening head, knowing he was already close.

"Please…" He tightened his grasp until it almost hurt. "Finish this."

I obeyed without hesitation, taking him in once more,

46

sucking and licking, stroking him, tasting him. I let him dictate the pace, hoping that once I'd satisfied him, he'd return the favor.

Yakolev threw his head back and pushed roughly into my mouth. I caught my breath, dug my fingers into his buttocks and sucked hard until he climaxed and his seed swept down my throat. I swallowed until he was spent, until his legs trembled and he slid down the wall with a long, shuddering sigh.

I sat back on my heels and looked at him, my own needs forgotten for the moment. He stared back, lips parted, chest rising and falling while he caught his breath. "Come here."

I shuffled forward on my knees until I knelt between his parted legs.

He touched my face, fingers trailing along my jaw, while he pressed his thumb to my mouth. I licked it. He closed his eyes and shivered.

"I was right to want you."

I didn't reply. I couldn't find words that fit. I regarded him mutely while he continued his leisurely exploration. He stayed his hand on my chest and flicked his thumb over my nipple until it rose in a tight, tense bud. Then, he leaned toward me and closed his lips around it, tickling it with the tip of his tongue until I trembled and clutched his shoulders. He moved lower, trailing his lips over my skin, dipping his tongue into my navel.

"Do you like what I'm doing to you?" Yakolev lifted his head and smiled.

I nodded and squeezed his shoulders once more, letting my fingers glide over his warm skin. I faltered when he closed his mouth over my erection, enveloping me in heat. He pushed me until I was on my back, on the floor. Yakolev drew away and studied me in silence. "I don't know what to do with you, where to start. You have so much that I want."

He edged forward, propped up on his arms while he loomed over me, his rapidly swelling member pressed to mine. Then he ducked to kiss me, catching my bottom lip between his teeth, pausing then kissing me again in teasing little sips. I pushed my hips toward his and clutched his arse, wanting him closer, desperate to resolve the rising tension in my loins. Moisture trickled onto my belly, reminding me of how little it would take to send me over the edge, how only the slightest of touches or shift of his hips over mine could set me alight.

"No, this won't do." He rocked back on his heels, stood and pulled me to my feet. "Bed, now."

I scrambled onto the low mattress. Yakolev dug into a small chest at the foot of the bed and produced a small bottle before kneeling on the bed between my legs. "I want to fuck you." His voice was hoarse.

"Yes."

He undid the stopper and poured liquid into his cupped palm. He dipped his fingers into the oil, then applied them to my opening, tracing a careful circle with the warm fluid before breaching, dabbing inwards, circling and easing further. He bit his lip and slipped a cautious digit into me. I rose to his touch, startled that he'd touched something inside that made me burn for more. He applied more oil to his cock and positioned it at my entrance.

I reached for him.

Yakolev plunged into me without preamble. His first, desperate thrust almost lifted me from the bed. I cried out, more from surprise than anything else, then pulled him close. He stooped to kiss me, devouring me with his mouth before moving on to my throat, which he peppered with sharp little bites while he moved relentlessly inside me.

His head dropped forward, dark hair falling over his forehead. The lamplight found fire in it while I found fire in every move he made. I seized his hair, pulled his face back to mine and demanded his attention. I wanted his lips crushing mine. He granted my unspoken wish, each kiss, each heated sweep of his tongue, followed by a low, feral growl. I was well and truly taken.

"So…close…" Yakolev nipped my ear. "You?"

"Very." It was all I could choke out before my balls tightened and I climaxed with a cry.

Yakolev glided in once more. He held my chin in one hand, slid his thumb over my lip and smiled. "Beautiful."

I hadn't the wit to reply but I caught him when he shuddered and fell into my arms, his seed spilling into me.

We recovered in a silence fractured by our slowing breaths. Yakolev didn't move, apart from to reach up and curl his fingers into my hair. He rested his head on my chest, turning once to brush his lips over a nipple before collapsing into semi-consciousness again.

I stroked his shoulders, reveling in the feel of his skin beneath my fingertips. He felt as if he belonged there. It certainly didn't feel as if I'd made a deal with the devil. The heat of the evening receded, pushed away by a cool breeze that drifted idly through the open window. Beyond the walls, Bukhara settled into a restless silence. I didn't want to move, to leave that tiny room or that narrow bed. I didn't want Yakolev to move, but he did, rolling off me to the side. He propped himself up on his elbow and grinned, his eyes suddenly alive with devilry. "You were well worth the risk, my friend."

"I'm glad to hear it. I just hope that the Emir doesn't see fit to throw you into the Pit for your insolence."

"He won't." He pushed the hair back from my forehead and planted a kiss there.

"Your confidence is breathtaking. Just be careful."

"Captain O'Riordan, I do believe you care."

"Of course I do. He's a madman. The dungeon is a terrible place. You would not survive."

"It won't happen." Yakolev settled beside me, throwing one leg over mine. "If it does, I'll have memories of this night." He brushed his lips over my skin. "Will you stay?"

I rolled over to face him. His eyes were dark, unfathomable. I had no idea what secrets dwelt there. I only knew that I wanted to find out.

"Yes." We'd only have this one night, this oasis.

"Good." He reached for me and drew me to him once more.

* * * *

I woke at dawn, to the drift of pale light through the window and the morning call to prayer. A rooster called out from somewhere, setting off a chorus of dogs. Yakolev stirred behind me, pressing closer, tightening his hold around my waist.

"Good morning." His breath was warm on my skin. "Are you all right?"

"Exhausted, battered, sated. Yes, I'm fine." Every part of me ached, felt used…in a good way, in a way that left me content. "But I should go, before Akmal thinks you've murdered me."

Yakolev laughed softly. "Probably wise. Beside which, I have another audience today."

I turned over and glanced at him. "Be careful." I meant it.

"I will." He caught my face between his hands and kissed me. "You had better go or I might be tempted."

"Yes." My cock had already responded to his touch. "Same here." I reluctantly eased away from him and stood up, aware that he watched me while I retrieved my clothes from the tangle of robes on the floor. "Is there water? I'd like to wash."

"There's a jug on the table, and a bowl. You should find some soap beside it." Yakolev settled back against the bolster, hands linked across his stomach.

I poured tepid water into a chipped porcelain bowl and wet the small, dried nub of soap, working it into a thin lather. I splashed water on my face and torso, before applying the soap. I shivered when the breeze brushed my damp skin.

"That's a fine sight." The bedclothes rustled when Yakolev got out of bed and padded across the floor. "Perhaps I shouldn't let you leave."

"I think I should."

He slid his arms around my waist. His erection pressed between my buttocks. My resolve came close to crumbling.

"No, I need to go."

His sigh was hot on the back of my neck. "I suppose you'd better." He stepped away and picked up his clothes.

I finished washing and dressed.

"Can I see you again?" Yakolev touched my arm.

"Yes."

He smiled. "Tell me where you're staying. I'll send word."

I told him then walked toward the door when all I wanted to do was change direction, grab him and fall back onto the bed.

"Gabriel."

I turned around.

Yakolev took my hand. "I *will* send for you. I promise."

"I'll look forward to it…Valentin."

His fingers slid away slowly. "Take care."

"You're the one who needs to be careful."

"I will. I promise." His smile was more uncertain.

His sudden loss of confidence scared me a bit. I took a step back, seized his chin and kissed him before walking away.

51

Chapter Five

I took my time strolling along the still quiet streets. The only sign of life was in the bazaar where stallholders were already setting out their wares for the day. I stopped by the fruit stand and bought some grapes before heading back to Akmal's place. I knew he'd be waiting, anxious that I'd survived the night.

"Praise be to Allah." He flung the door open and ushered me into the house. "I was beginning to worry."

"I'm fine." I handed him the grapes. "I survived, Yakolev survived. It was a pleasant way to pass the time."

He shook his head. "You are mad."

"I'm happy, safe and very, very tired."

"And I'm very relieved." He steered me toward the staircase. "You must rest. You look exhausted."

I fought the urge to grin, remembering why I was exhausted. "I could sleep."

"Then sleep. I'll make sure you're not disturbed."

"Thank you, my friend."

"I'm just glad you made it back in one piece."

I stumbled up the stairs to the refuge of my room. It was a relief to strip out of my clothes and fall, exhausted into the empty bed.

* * * *

I woke at midday, disappointed at finding myself in an empty bed. I'd half expected to wake to find Valentin there. I rolled onto my back and stared at the ceiling. He'd ignited something in me. I wasn't sure what, but I knew that I wanted more.

I rose and dressed, still groggy. Someone had left water in a basin on the small table. I splashed some on my face and raked my fingers over the day-old stubble. I couldn't be bothered to risk the cut-throat razor. I had no intention of going anywhere. Unease lurked in the pit of my stomach. My grandmother had called it a gift, this sense of dread that some of the O'Riordan's seem to own. Me, I just called it rubbish and put it down to tiredness.

I found Akmal in the courtyard, sitting in the shade.

"Ah, you've decided to join us."

I slumped onto a chair. "I decided it would be a waste of a day to sleep. I don't like wasting days."

"No, you never did." He turned and called to his wife, ordering tea and food.

A moment later, she peered through the kitchen door and replied that food was on the way.

"She is a good woman, my wife." Akmal grinned and patted my hand. "Are you sure you won't think of finding a good woman?"

"No, thank you. I prefer things the way they are. If I have to die a lonely old man, I'll be all right with that."

"I hope you live long enough to die an old man, my friend."

"So do I." The outlook wasn't good. My mission was close to failure, I'd sold my soul to an enemy in exchange for a request that had fallen on deaf ears. I did not relish returning to India empty-handed. At that moment, I did not relish returning to India at all.

"Don't worry. You are a clever man. You will survive." He glanced up when Farrukh reappeared in the courtyard, bearing a tray laden with food, one of his daughters trailed behind her carrying another. Farrukh set the tray on the low table with a smile and took the other from her daughter.

"You missed breakfast," she admonished me. "Now you must eat. There's plenty here." She nudged her husband's shoulder. "You make sure our guest eats. He looks too thin."

Akmal laughed and rested his hand on his ample belly. "Are you trying to fatten him up?"

"He is too thin," she chided. "He will waste away."

"All right, I'll eat. As it happens, this looks splendid." I eyed the pile of warm, flat slabs of bread.

Farrukh dimpled, blushed and returned to the house.

"Go on." Akmal pushed a bowl of rice toward me. "Eat and tell me about your Russian friend."

I tore off a piece of bread and dipped it into the honey. The fragrance of blossoms drifted up to meet me. The sweetness melted on my tongue. "What can I tell you that wouldn't be indecent?"

"Did he treat you well?"

My cheeks burnt when memories of the previous evening rushed back. "Yes, he did. He was an excellent host."

And lover, don't forget that.

Akmal raised an eyebrow. "Really?"

"Really." I helped myself to some rice and some stew. The spices stung my tongue. "He was good company."

"What am I going to do with you? If they find out what you did…"

"No one will. Yakolev won't say anything, he'd be in as much trouble as me if he told his superiors."

"I suppose not." Akmal plucked some grapes from a beaten metal platter. "What will you do now?"

"I don't know. Yakolev tells me that the Emir refused his request. That he has nothing to fear from the British. After Kabul, he doesn't think he will be attacked. I'm afraid that he's probably right. I fear for their lives, I don't think they have long to live. Nor does Yakolev. He thinks that Bukhara will be dangerous for foreigners. That I should leave while I still can."

"Will you?"

"I'll wait and see what happens. I obviously can't free them, especially if he decides to throw them into the Pit again. Whatever happens now, it's clear I'll be returning to

54

India empty-handed."

"It is better for you to return to India empty-handed, than not to return at all. I think Yakolev could be right. It won't be safe for you…or him. Perhaps you should go while you can."

How did I tell him that I didn't want to leave until I'd seen Valentin once more? I wanted to assure myself that he was all right, that he would be safe, that he would survive his encounter with Nasrullah. "Let me think about it. I don't want to go until I'm absolutely certain that there's nothing more I can do."

"You are stubborn."

"I am clinging to hope for a miracle."

Akmal sighed theatrically. "All right. But I suggest you stay here, where you are safe. I will see what I can find out."

"I want to see Yakolev again."

"You are a fool. Are you so desperate that you would risk your life just for another night with him?"

I considered the question and helped myself to a piece of cheese. "Don't worry, I'll grow that damned beard back so at least I look like Rashid again."

He laughed. "You must be interested if you're willing to put up with that misery just to see him. I don't want him hurting you."

"He won't." I attacked a bowl of rice with conviction and that put an end to that particular conversation.

＊ ＊ ＊ ＊

"Gabriel, wake up." Akmal's voice intruded on a dream, one about home…or at least I thought it was home. It was all green and cool one moment, then covered in snow the next.

"What time is it?" I opened my eyes to a soft shred of light spilling through the open window. Lunch had made me sleepy and now it appeared to be early evening.

Akmal shrugged. "Your spy is here to see you. He's

waiting in the courtyard."

"Val...Yakolev is here?" I hadn't expected to see him so soon. I wasn't sure I was up to another night of his ravishments.

"He has news. Important news."

"All right." I sat up, and groped for my robe, reluctant to put it on in the summer heat. "Any idea what?"

"No. He doesn't look happy. He doesn't look like a man who's paying a visit on a lover."

I glared at him. "One night, Akmal. That's all. My debt to him is paid."

"If you say so." Akmal walked to the door. "I'll tell him you'll be down in a minute, and Farrukh will bring you both some tea." He disappeared, leaving me to finish getting dressed. I scrambled into the soft house slippers Akmal had given me then hurried down the staircase.

I found Yakolev standing beside the fountain in the courtyard. He turned when I walked out of the door.

"O'Riordan." His voice was cold, the passionate, wild lover of the previous night hidden away somewhere.

"Yakolev." I gestured toward the low bench beneath the portico. "Will you have a seat? Farrukh will bring us some tea."

"Fine." He strode toward the shade. I watched him, seeking out the body I'd worshiped beneath the swirl of white robes. He sank onto the bench and crossed his legs.

"This is no invitation or social call, is it?" I joined him on the bench, sitting far enough away to avoid temptation. "What's wrong?" The unease I'd felt earlier returned tenfold.

"The Emir has decided that Stoddart and Connolly are to be executed in the morning."

The words were delivered like punches. I caught my breath and tried to reply. "What?"

"He told me that, since he was in no danger from the British, he was going to rid himself of the infidels. He has no further need for them."

"Jesus."

The rattle of porcelain on metal heralded Farrukh's approach. She slid the tray onto the bench wordlessly and left on a shy smile. I poured the tea and pushed a plate of sweetmeats toward Valentin, who waved them away with a weary hand.

"I'm sorry. I hate to be the one to have to tell you this news. But I thought you'd want to know as soon as possible."

I stared blankly into my tea and set my cup down. "Thank you. Then that's it. I can think of no miracle, no magic way to free them."

Valentin moved his hand across the carpeted bench and touched mine. "I wish I'd been able to help, to persuade him. I did try today, you know. When he told me what he'd decided. I really tried. Told him that it was still risky, that Britain would not forget." He ran his other hand through his already tousled hair. "But he is clearly in one of his moods and not only is he Emir of Bukhara, he is also Emperor of the world today."

I wound my fingers through his. "It's all right. You didn't have to say anything to him. I don't want you to risk your own neck."

His eyes were dark and unreadable. What good-natured devilry had once dwelt there, had disappeared. "It is done. I just needed you to know that I *did* try."

"Then I am once again in your debt."

He managed a smile then. A brief flicker of light and memories returned. "I shall remember to collect. Just not tonight. I am exhausted. I need to sleep."

"I have slept most of the day. I doubt that I will sleep tonight." I took a deep breath. "Where is this execution to take place? If nothing else, I need to bear witness, so at least I can give my employers a first-hand account of the end."

"In the square in front of the Ark. I will come for you in the morning. You do not need to see this on your own. I will be there."

I swallowed at the sudden hard lump in my throat. "Thank

you." I resisted the urge to seek his touch once more. I saw no more passionate nights in our future. The business was nearly done and I would have to leave Bukhara.

Valentin downed his tea swiftly and rose. "I'll leave you in peace. Try to rest, Gabriel. You'll need your wits about you."

"I know." I stood. "I'll see you out."

"Thanks. Sorry I couldn't stay longer. I'm not sure that your friends would want a stranger here."

"They are good people. Very good people."

He gave me the ghost of a grin. "Who know a good man when they see one."

I led him across the courtyard to the short shadowy hall in the house beyond. Valentin paused beside the door and curled his hand around my shoulder. "I'm glad you're in a safe place and you're being looked after. But please be careful."

I scratched the day's worth of stubble on my chin. "Don't worry, Akmal has already lectured me sternly on things. He has persuaded me to resume my holy man guise."

"So you are to be reunited with the dreaded beard." He grinned and touched my cheek. "I'm not sure I like that."

"I don't, but Akmal is right."

"I'd better go. Try and sleep." He pressed his lips to my forehead for a moment and sighed. "I'll see you in the morning." He opened the door and slipped out onto the silent street. I leaned against the wall and wrapped my shaking hands around the voluminous fabric of my robe.

I returned to the courtyard.

"Is everything all right?" Akmal asked when I sank onto the bench.

"No. It seems that Stoddart and Connolly are to be executed in the morning." I rubbed my eyes. "I shall have to go. Yakolev will come for me. We'll go together."

Akmal muttered something very much like a curse. "The Emir is a fool."

"A mad fool. God, those poor men."

"From what I've heard about the Pit, they may welcome death."

I glanced at him. "What have you heard?"

He reached for his tea. "It's a hole in the ground, nothing more. Every day, the guards throw scorpions, insects and rats onto the prisoners, and who knows what else. Any man would go mad in such a place."

"Yes." My stomach churned. "I suppose being beheaded would be a welcome alternative. I'd be surprised if either of them were in their right minds after all this time."

Akmal shook his head. "It wouldn't surprise me. Most men do go mad after a while."

I tried not to think about how it would've been for them in an airless, dark hole in the relentless desert heat. I didn't want to witness their death, no matter what a mercy it might have been. On top of that, there was the bitter taste of my failure. I would be returning to India with my tail between my legs.

* * * *

A small crowd had already gathered in the open space beneath the solid, forbidding walls of the Ark. An air of dark expectation dulled the brilliance of the morning. Valentin stood beside me, pressed close by the weight of the crowd. His fingertips brushed mine. I wanted to grip his arm, anything to release the tension that churned inside me.

A low murmur rippled through the crowd like a chill wind, then a collective catch of breath when two men, hands bound, were led into the square. In an instant, their bounds were cut and digging implements were thrust into their hands. I couldn't hear the words that followed, but moments later, they both started digging, setting pale clouds of dust adrift in the breeze.

Valentin's fingers tightened around mine. "Jesus, they're having to dig their own damn graves."

The unease I'd felt for the last day or so unfurled inside me. I wanted to be sick. I wanted to be anywhere else. The gathering fell into a silence broken only by the sound of the tools grinding into dirt and the incongruously sweet trill of a bird somewhere beyond the square. After a while, both men stepped back. Another order, this one audible, compelled them to drop to their knees. I wanted to be sick. I would've run had Valentin not been there.

Whether they were allowed to speak, I did not know. The man who I vaguely recognized as Stoddart launched into a vehement tirade against the Emir. All of which I wanted to cheer. Instead I bit my lip and glanced away when the Executioner's blade ended the speech with one brutal sweep of his sword.

Valentin pressed closer. I swallowed my rising nausea.

The executioner turned to Connolly. This time, his voice was clear.

"The Emir has graciously decreed that your life will be spared."

A startled whisper moved through the crowd like electricity. Something like hope rose inside me.

"If you renounce your infidel ways and embrace Islam."

Connolly cleared his throat and spoke. "Colonel Stoddart has been a Mussulman for three years and you have killed him. I will not become one and I am ready to die." Then, with a grace beyond dignity he extended his neck, clearly ready to embrace death. My eyes burnt and I dashed the tears away before anyone could notice.

The executioner's sword glinted in the sunlight then flashed when it swept downward. Connolly's head dropped unceremoniously onto the dirt while his blood mingled with that of his compatriot's. I turned away, unable to watch any more. I wanted to be far away from there. I pushed through the stunned crowd, gasping for air. I didn't stop until I reached the edge of the square.

"Gabriel." Valentin caught my arm. "I'm sorry."

I took a deep breath and faced him. "It's all right. I'll be fine. It won't be easy to forget the bloody reminder of my failure, but I'll do it."

"I don't quite know what to say. It was a sickening, barbaric act."

"I've come to expect nothing less. But this is the worst of all the things I have seen since I started this…this…mess of a job."

"And me." He sighed and stared at his hands. "Will you come back to the lodging with me?"

In my weakness I could think of nothing better than losing myself in the comfort of someone's arms, even if it was nothing more than empty relief. "Yes."

"Come on then." His voice was gentle.

We walked in silence through the streets. There was no sense of urgency this time, no desperate need to slake desire. When we reached the house, Valentin led me up the stairs without a word.

"Come here." This time the order was gently spoken.

I stood before him, still clothed and waiting for his next move, unsure whether my body would respond to his touch. He pulled me close, sliding his arms around my waist. He held me without speaking, his breath warm against my cheek while he stroked my hair. "I'm sorry I can offer nothing but my body, as you offered yours."

"It's a generous offer but I'm not sure I…"

"It's all right." He steered me toward the bed, lay down and pulled me down beside him. "Sometimes, that's not what's needed."

I settled into the crook of his arm readily enough. Despite the heat of the day, a chill had crept into my veins. I needed the physical comfort of another being. I just needed to be held.

Valentin kept stroking my hair, slowing as his breathing deepened toward sleep. I closed my eyes and huddled closer, finding comfort in his touch. I would've happily remained there forever. As it was, I drifted off, seeking refuge in the silence of a dreamless slumber.

* * * *

I woke to find Valentin curled around me. At some point, he'd shed his robes and slept naked, one leg thrown over mine. It seemed that even in sleep, he needed to exercise some sort of authority. I slipped carefully from his arms and undressed before returning to the bed. I wanted to spend as much time there as I could, knowing that I would soon be leaving Bukhara and would never see him again. For some reason, the thought of not seeing Valentin again upset me. Given the inauspicious beginning to our friendship, it seemed…strange.

Valentin huddled closer. The feel of his skin on mine ignited desires I hadn't been able to feel earlier. I turned in his arms and touched his face.

"What do you want?" His voice was drowsy but he raised his leg, brushing it over mine. "I think I can guess."

I took his hand and guided it down to my cock.

Valentin grinned, suddenly awake. His eyes full of fire and light. He rolled onto me without preamble, pressing me down onto the yielding mattress. "I can take care of that for you."

"Thank you." I pulled him closer, raising my hips to meet his until we moved in concord, simple friction bringing me perilously close to release.

After a few, frantic moments of grappling, Valentin sat back on his heels and reached for the oil. "I want to be inside you."

"Yes. I want that too." It scared me how much I wanted that, wanted *him*.

He applied the oil to himself and to me. "Good." He was surprisingly gentle after those heated minutes beforehand. Now and then, he'd pause in his ministrations, lean down, then move his lips over my fevered skin. Every touch made me more desperate for him.

I reached for him, grasping his shoulders as he lowered himself toward me and positioned his cock at my entrance.

He ducked his head to give me a biting kiss before slowly easing into me. I couldn't take my gaze from his face. His hair flopped over his brow. I lifted my hand and brushed it away from his eyes. He turned and kissed my palm. Something in that simple gesture lost me forever. For those few brief moments, everything else was forgotten.

* * * *

"Will you leave Bukhara now, while you still can?" Valentin brushed a crease from the sleeve of my robe.

"Yes. I'll head back with my tail between my legs and give my superiors an account of what happened. That's all I can do."

He kissed my forehead. "Stay safe. I don't suppose our paths will cross again."

I swallowed, fighting the knowledge that he was right. Our game was played on too big a field. "No." I put my hand on the door, ready to step out into the street. "I don't suppose they will. Look after yourself, Valentin and try not to cross the Emir."

"I won't."

"Goodbye." I walked away and didn't look back.

Chapter Six

I secured my pack to the saddle then tightened the girth. The courtyard was still cool in the soft, violet shadows of morning. I tried not to think of the journey ahead. Instead I thought of the beyond, of peace and quiet in the cottage, of sitting with a good book and a glass of whiskey before a peat fire. When I got to Calcutta, I was going to resign my commission. Bukhara was the last straw.

"Gabriel!" Akmal strode into the courtyard, his face pale.

The alarm in his voice roused a primal worry inside me. I rested a shaking hand on the horse's rump and waited. "What is it?"

"Your Russian friend. It seems the Emir has taken a dislike to him."

"What do you mean?"

"He's been thrown in the Pit."

The worry became something tangible, a smack in the gut. "For doing what?"

Akmal shrugged. "No one knows. Only that he had an audience with the Emir which ended badly and he was taken away."

"Jesus." I leaned against the horse's flank, paralyzed by the dark possibilities. Every sane voice inside me urged me to leave.

I couldn't.

I unstrapped my bags from the saddle and unfastened the girth. "All right, change of plan. I need to think of a way to get him out of there."

"Are you mad? You should leave Bukhara while you still can."

I scratched at the wretched growth of beard I'd been cultivating over the previous few days. "No, I can't do that. I failed Stoddart and Connolly, I'm not going to fail him."

"But why save him? Why risk your life for an enemy?"

"Because he took a big risk asking the Emir to release Stoddart and Connolly into his custody. For all we know, that's why he's being punished."

"What do you propose to do? What miracle did you have in mind, my friend?"

I pulled the saddle from the horse's back then removed the bridle. "I don't know. Give me some time to think." I had to come up with something. "I can't ride away from Bukhara with a clear conscience knowing Valentin could be killed."

Akmal shook his head and retrieved my saddle. "Are you sure there isn't more to it than some foolish notion of honor?"

"I'm sure." I closed the stable door.

Akmal shook his head. "You British, I will never understand you."

"I have nothing to lose. I have every intention of resigning my commission when I return to India. This latest failure has just reminded me that this is a foolish and dangerous game that I'm tired of playing. Valentin is no different than I am. He just happens to work for a country that has different interests to ours." I followed Akmal back into the house. "I need to think."

"Fine. But I'll not risk my life or that of my family's to help. I can give you information but that is all."

I patted his shoulder. "I wouldn't dream of asking you to risk anything. This mission is entirely my own."

"Thank you. I just wish you'd reconsider."

"I can't do that. I'd do the same if you were in Valentin's place."

He sighed. "Yes, I know you would. Your loyalty is to be commended. I understand why you feel you must do this. I just don't want to lose a friend, that's all."

"If I can't think of a sensible way to get Valentin out of there, I won't do anything foolish."

"Good." He grinned. "Now I will go and tell Farrukh that she can continue to spoil you with good food. She will be pleased."

"The good food will help. Thank you." I climbed the stairs, anxious to retreat to my room to think.

* * * *

I hated that beard. The June heat made its presence more than a simple annoyance. But I needed it.

"Do I look like a scholar of Islam?" I asked Akmal.

He surveyed me over the rim of his tea cup. "I think you could pass for one, yes. What did you have in mind?"

"I want an audience with the Emir. The Russian gentleman he has imprisoned is my student. He came to me seeking instruction in Islam in order to encourage his countrymen to do the same, so they had a better understanding of the local culture." I raised my cup to Akmal. "Does that seem like a convincing enough story?"

He set his tea down and plucked a handful of grapes from a bowl. "It sounds plausible. And it wouldn't be the first time you've used this disguise. How well do you know the Koran now?"

"Backwards. I can recite chapter and verse."

"But can you discuss it with a man of the faith?"

"I've discussed it with you many a time, haven't I?"

Akmal laughed. "Yes you have, my friend. I think you can do this. I only hope that you succeed."

"So do I. Now all I need to do is get an audience with the bastard."

"I will see what I can do."

* * * *

The Emir of the Khanate of Bukhara glared at me with ferocious black eyes. He lifted one idle, plump hand and

66

waved languidly at a passing fly. Almost instantly, a fawning attendant shooed the impertinent insect away with a horsetail swatter.

"Why" — he leaned forward and reached for a metal goblet — "would you wish to instruct an infidel in the ways of Islam?"

I remained still, resting on my heels as I knelt before him. "Because he wanted to learn. In order to understand our ways and learn to respect them." I hoped I looked calmer than I felt. Inside my churning guts argued with the tea I had been offered once ushered into his presence.

"Did you believe his intentions to be honorable?"

I swallowed. "Yes, I do, Your Serene Highness. He appeared to be most enthusiastic. He had even obtained a copy of the Koran and had begun to teach himself. I believe that demonstrates the integrity of his intentions. As you yourself know, it is not something to be taken lightly."

The Emir raked his fingers through his beard. "What will you teach him?"

"Everything, Your Serene Highness. He told me that he wanted to learn everything. He feels that he was leading a less than wholesome life and he wants deliverance and mercy. He is certainly single-minded enough to learn. I do not believe he is doing this as a means of gaining your favor."

"I didn't ask what you didn't believe." He snapped, his expression suddenly far from serene. The attendant backed away a few places, clutching the horse tail.

I took a deep breath and curled my hands into the folds of my robe. "With your permission, I wish to take him to my village. There he will be hidden away from the temptations of Bukhara. I think it's best that he is in a place where there are no distractions, where he can lead a simple, pious life, such as I lead." Had I believed in a God, or Allah, or whoever, I was sure I was destined to burn in hell for my lies.

His Serene Highness chewed thoughtfully on the end of

his beard. The receiving chamber fell into a silence broken only by the sporadic hum of the errant fly, which seemed determined to make its presence felt. The attendant set the swatter down and poured more tea for us both. I thought it imprudent to wave him away. The last thing I wanted was more fuel for my turbulent guts. I picked up the cup with as steady a hand as I could manage and took a tentative sip.

The Emir nodded and pushed a plate of sweetmeats toward me. The scent of rosewater and pistachios confronted me. "You are a very wise and learned man, sir." He leaned back and offered me a knowing smile, his face suddenly transformed by an expression of such benevolence it was almost impossible to believe him capable of the atrocities he'd committed. "Leave me now and let me consider your proposal. I believe that it has some merit."

I rocked back on my heels and rose, remembering to bow my way out of his presence. "Thank you, Your Serene Highness. I would be most grateful for your consideration."

"To save the soul of an infidel is a good thing." His grin was wolfish. "To save the soul of an infidel who could be of much use to us would be even better. I will send word when I have made my decision."

I backed away until I found the door. Another attendant opened it for me and allowed me to depart with my head still intact.

* * * *

"It's been two weeks. How long does the bastard need?" I pushed my plate away and glanced across the courtyard when a bird settled onto the lip of the fountain and started singing.

Akmal leaned across and patted my hand. "God willing, you will hear soon. It may be that the Emir has more pressing matters to attend to. The wellbeing of one Russian officer will mean little to him."

I tugged at my beard, hating it, wanting to be away from

the sullen heat of Bukhara in July. "He is still alive, isn't he?"

"The last I heard, yes. He obviously is not in the best of spirits, but he is alive." Akmal's glance slid away.

"What aren't you telling me?"

"You know it is not a good place. He has been there for three weeks. Three weeks in a hole in the ground with nothing but scorpions and rats for company. He will not be well. If you succeed in your mission, you won't be able to leave here until he is well enough to travel."

I tried to imagine what condition Valentin would be in. He would've been treated appallingly, the unsanitary conditions he would've had to endure would have been unspeakable, far beyond the realm of my experience, and I'd been in some very bad places. "If he is freed, I'll take him back to his lodgings and care for him myself. I don't want to risk your life by bringing him here."

Akmal exhaled audibly. "I think that would be best. Thank you for your consideration, my friend. If you do that, I will make sure that you have everything you need. I'll make sure you have plenty to eat and if medicines are needed, I can get those for you too."

My heart expanded in a rush of relief and warmth. "You are a good man. I will never be able to repay you for your kindness."

"There is no need. As I've said many times before, thanks to you, my family and I have a good life here. In spite of the Emir. I keep my head down, do my job and I'm left in peace."

"Very well. I accept your offer. Let's just hope that the bastard has a rare moment of compassion and lets Valentin go."

We sat in silence. I glanced down at the array of dishes Farrukh had provided for us and wished for nothing more than a plate of roast beef and a bottle of good wine. I'd had enough of Bukhara in more ways than one. I helped myself to some of the crumbling white cheese, sprinkling it onto a slab of the ubiquitous flat bread. The first thing I would do when I got home, I decided, was to tuck into a fine dinner, then I would settle into my favorite chair in front of the fireplace with a good book. It could rain all it liked, because I didn't plan on going anywhere. Perhaps there would be whiskey too, the best Irish I could find. I could drink myself into oblivion and forget Bukhara and my failures.

Farrukh hurried into the courtyard. She bent low and whispered frantically to her husband, whilst casting uneasy glances in my direction. I watched them unashamedly, knowing that there was news. It could be nothing else. After a moment, she gave me an uncertain smile and returned to the house.

Akmal set down his bowl of rice and smiled. "Word has arrived from the Emir. The prisoner will be released into your custody when you present yourself to the Head of the Household Guard at the entrance to The Ark."

I scrambled to my feet, suddenly breathless and shaking. "I don't know whether to be relieved or worried."

"Be neither. Be calm. You need to keep your wits about you." He strode toward the doorway. "I will ask Farrukh to get some things together and arrange for them to be taken to the lodgings. You just go and rescue your Russian friend."

"Thank you, my friend." I took deep breath and wiped my suddenly sweaty palms on my robe. It took everything I had not to rush out of the door. Instead, I took another deep breath, ran up the stairs and gathered a few things together. There would be plenty of time to rest later.

* * * *

The Head of the Emir's Household Guard smothered a yawn. "He is being brought to you now."

"Thank you." I stood in the relentless sun and hoped that I looked calmer than I felt.

The shuffle of feet heralded the arrival of someone, or more than one. I wasn't sure. I raised my head and glanced toward the far side of the courtyard. Two guards appeared in an archway, dragging someone between them. Only the glint of sunlight on brown hair gave me any indication that the wasted creature staggering toward me was Valentin. I bit my lip, anxious to conceal my shock. My hands trembled. I hid them in my robe.

After an agony of waiting, he stood before me, clutching his stomach and held up only by the brutal grip of a guard's arm. He regarded me with blank eyes.

"Mr Yakolev, do you remember me? I am Rashid. Your tutor." I made each word clear, hoping that somewhere inside him, he would get the message.

Silence weighed heavily on the moment. Valentin slowly lifted his head and his lips twitched in the semblance of a smile. "Of course I remember you, kind sir. Why are you here?"

"His Serene Highness has graciously released you into my care so that you may continue your education. So that you may embrace the ways of Islam."

"Ah yes. Thank you. I'm relieved to see you. Will you be looking after me?"

I strained to hear the words that crawled from between his cracked lips. "Yes. I'm taking you back to your lodgings and when you are well enough to travel, I will take you to my village, where you may learn without distraction."

One of the guards released his arm and the other shoved him forward until he tumbled toward me. I caught him, struggling to bear the weight of him and the fetid miasma that surrounded him. My eyes watered and I breathed through my mouth, not wanting to do any more than that. "Let's get you home, sir."

"Thank you," he rasped, clutching my sleeve with a hand that resembled a pale, bony claw, while he held his other arm over his stomach, as if shielding himself from pain.

I forced myself to look at the Head of the Household Guard. "His Serene Highness is most merciful. Kindly convey my humble gratitude for his generosity. I wish him many more years. Bukhara will only benefit from his strength and wisdom."

The Guard nodded and waved me away as if he were swatting at a persistent fly.

I slid my arm around Valentin's waist and steered him toward the exit and freedom.

We staggered away from the Ark, each labored step taking us closer to freedom. Valentin leaned heavily on me as we made our way to the street, leaving the fortress walls towering behind us. People gave us horrified stares and wide berths and I was grateful that they hurried away, casting uneasy glances over their shoulders. A sea of whispers trailed in our wake. I ignored them and tried to make sense of the remnants of the man I'd been given. There was nothing left of the passionate, demanding lover. Nothing left of the man whose kiss haunted me, left me wanting more. The wreckage I bore reeked of piss and filth. His unshaven beard crawled with vermin and the skin beneath his dull, gray eyes was black under the grime of three weeks' confinement. For the briefest of foolish moments, I wanted nothing more than to turn around, grab a sword and lay waste to the Emir for what he had done. Instead, I tightened my grip around Valentin's waist and helped him to the relative safety of his house.

When we had made our way some distance away from the Ark, he paused and squeezed my arm. He glanced over his shoulder then reached into the tattered remains of his shirt. "Here," he whispered. "Take this. I found it." He pressed a book into my hands. "Hurry. Hide it."

I slid it into my robe without looking, hoping it wasn't as riddled with vermin as its bearer was. "What is it?"

"A prayer book. It has things written in it. I couldn't read...it was too dark. It belonged to Connelly, I think.

"Bloody hell." I shook, almost afraid that it would bring ill fortune. Perhaps it had brought the two men some comfort in their darkest days, but perhaps it was part of their ill fortune.

Valentin slumped against me. "Hurry, please...so...so..."

"All right, we're nearly there. Don't worry, I'll look after you." I braced myself to bear his weight once more and guided him along the narrow, silent street.

Once in the privacy of the courtyard, I sat Valentin down carefully on the edge of the fountain and stripped the filthy, tattered remnants of his clothes away. I tossed them aside into a corner. "I need to clean you. Stay there."

"I haven't the strength to go anywhere. Don't worry." A trace of humor colored his voice.

"Do you know who I am?" I sorted through my bag and pulled a cloth and shaving gear out.

"Gabriel. My angel Gabriel come to save me." Valentin's eyes burnt with sudden emotion. "God bless you."

I swallowed at the sudden lump in my throat. "I've been called many things in my life, but never an angel."

He lifted his hand then let it fall to his side, as if it were too much of an effort to do anything more. "You are."

I made a lather in the small cup and dabbed my brush into it. "First thing we must do is get rid of this damnable filthy beard."

He tugged weakly at it. "Thank you. Now I understand your hatred of the bloody things. Miserable, aren't they?"

My own beard itched when I watched the vermin scurry through his. I hoped that my revulsion didn't show when I scraped the cutthroat blade over the growth. After some effort, which left me with a sore arm, and Valentin's face red and raw, the beard was gone and with it, its disgusting residents. Consigned to the same corner of the courtyard as the discarded robes. I would burn them later.

I then took a cloth, drenched it in cool water from the fountain and wiped it carefully over Valentin's skin. Each sweep revealed more of a mosaic of faded yellow and green bruises. "Christ, man. What did they do to you?"

He shrugged then dropped his head. "I don't remember." He drew in a deep breath and released it in a sigh. "I don't want to remember."

"It's all right. It's not important. I won't let them hurt you again. I promise."

"Angel."

"No, just Gabriel." I dabbed the cloth carefully around his private parts, relieved to see that no living thing had taken up residence there. Then I cleaned the dried feces from his legs, trying not to retch. I threw the cloth away and found another, working until no trace of prison filth remained.

Valentin shivered and grasped my arm. "Dear God, thank you. I can't tell you how good it feels just to be clean."

I sat down beside him and drew out a comb. "We're not quite there yet. I need to check your hair."

He dropped his head while I worked the comb through his greasy, tangled locks and found further evidence of lice. "Bugger." I searched through my things once more. "I can't abide creatures living in my hair. Luckily our Persian friends have the remedy." I found the bottle at the bottom of the pack. "Close your eyes."

Valentin complied. He curled his hands around the lip of the fountain while I poured water onto his hair.

"I've used it myself in the past. I won't travel without it."

"Are you thirsty? Shall I get you some water? Something else?"

"No, I'm all right for the moment. Just get those damned creatures out of my hair."

Satisfied that his hair was well drenched, I poured the liquid onto it and combed it through, wrestling with vicious tangles along the way. After a great deal of patience and effort, I had finished. Valentin was clean and his hair on the way to being vermin-free.

"Let's get you to bed." I took his arm and eased him to his feet. "What you need now more than anything is rest. I'll be here to look after you."

He leaned on me, sliding his arm around my waist when I led him toward the stairs. "How did you do it, Gabriel?"

"Do what?"

"Convince the Emir to set me free." His breath rattled as

we negotiated the narrow staircase.

"I'll tell you when you're recovered. Right now, you must sleep."

"Sleep would be nice. Promise me you won't leave me."

"I promise. I'm not going anywhere. Akmal is sending supplies. He'll get anything you need." I guided him toward the bedroom.

Valentin tumbled onto the bed. I wrenched the bedclothes from beneath him and covered him before opening the window. There wasn't much of a breeze, but the room was in need of an airing. I sank down onto the chair beside the window and sat quietly.

"Are you going to sit there?"

"Yes. Just in case you need me for anything. I'll only leave the room when Akmal arrives." I glanced down into the empty courtyard. The heat left the city in silence, only the trickle of water from the fountain offered the slightest of sounds.

"You will get bored." Valentin stifled a yawn, lifting one emaciated hand to his mouth.

"I'll be fine. I'm tired. I've hardly slept. I can use the rest."

"All right then." He rolled onto his side, pulled the thin sheet to his chin and closed his eyes. Before long, his breathing lengthened and his fingers eased their grip on the sheet. I propped my feet on the end of the bed and watched him sleep, trying to find the lover I'd left in that very room several weeks earlier.

The book he'd given me dug into my skin, reminding me of its presence. I withdrew it and sat with it on my lap for some time, afraid to open it, to see what was written there. The battered prayer book looked so innocuous—it was something that any devout Christian would have. My own mother had a Catholic Missal that she often read, her lips moving silently, while she sat beside the fire on a chilly evening. I took a deep breath and turned to a random page. The margins were full of scribbles, I could scarcely make out the writing and, after reading a few lines recounting the privations of my compatriots, I wished I hadn't.

My father once told me of a woman in the village who, simply by touching an object, could garner the emotions of the owner of that object. I remember being fascinated as a child that someone could possibly have that ability. As I stood and hurriedly shoved the wretched book into my bag, I was glad that I didn't share that dubious talent. I was certain that the feelings wrapped up in those desperate little scratches would be more than any living being could bear.

* * * *

"How is he?" Akmal gestured for his servants to set the boxes on the small table in what passed for the kitchen.

"Sleeping. He was filthy, so I spent a good hour bathing and shaving him and getting rid of the bloody lice." My skin crawled at the thought. "I'm just going to leave him to rest. I think that's what he needs more than anything."

"Yes. How is his health?"

"I don't know. He's very thin, very pale. He's clearly been beaten at some point because he's covered in old bruises. There's insect bites and some open sores."

"I brought some salve and some bandages, just in case." Akmal nodded toward one of the boxes. "There's plenty of food and some tea. If you need a doctor, just send Halim. I'm leaving him here with you. He can cook and run errands for you."

I glanced at the lad who had begun to unpack the supplies. "You don't have to do that."

"You will have your hands full. He is a good boy. Very discreet. You can trust him and he's a hard worker."

"Thank you."

Halim turned and offered me a shy grin. "I will look after you, the master thinks I am ready for the task."

I raised an eyebrow.

Akmal chuckled. "He is an ambitious boy. He sends his money to his family and has a kind heart. I can spare him for a little while."

"I'll see that he's handsomely rewarded."

"Thank you. You will have a loyal servant, I promise you."

"I appreciate it." I walked with him to the door. "If I need anything I'll let you know."

"I'll stop by tomorrow to see how things are going. If you have any problems in the meantime, just send Halim."

"Thank you." I glanced up the stairs, wondering if Valentin still slept.

"Go on." Akmal squeezed my shoulder. "Go and look after your lover. It's about time you found someone to love."

"What makes you think I love him?"

He smiled. "Would you have risked your life for him if you didn't?"

"I owed him. I always honor my debts, you know that."

"I know." He stepped into the street. "Take care, my friend. I will see you tomorrow."

I closed the door and retreated upstairs.

Valentin still slept. Still on his side. He snored noisily and a thin stream of dribble glistened on his chin. I fetched a damp cloth from the dressing table and gently wiped his face, hoping it would cool him. He stirred, whispering something, before rolling onto his back. His mouth fell open, releasing a cacophony of snores. I perched on the edge of the bed and stroked the hair from his forehead. His skin was clammy beneath my fingertips. The thin sheet clung to his frame, leaving me in no doubt that he had been starved during his captivity. Once more, I fought back a violent urge to murder the Emir. Instead I remained on the bed, guarding him, hoping that he'd recover from his ordeal.

* * * *

Valentin woke at dusk. I'd dozed off in my chair, lulled

to sleep earlier by Halim's constant singing as he tidied the house. The aroma of something cooking drifted through the open window, accompanied by the homely clatter of pots and pans.

"Hello." Valentin's voice was rusty.

"How are you?"

He struggled into a sitting position, propping himself up on wasted arms before collapsing against the wall. "Weak. I hate this."

"You'll get better and as soon as you do, we'll get out of this wretched place. I'll take you wherever you need to go."

"You'll what?" His eyes widened, showing more animation that they had up until that moment.

"I can't just leave you here. I told the Emir I was taking you to my village."

"Shouldn't you be heading back to India?"

"I should be, but why bother? I've failed. I'm only going to resign my commission and go home. I've had enough."

He covered up a barking cough. "What will you do?"

"Rest. Hide away in my cottage and spend my days reading and drinking whiskey. I think I've earned that right."

"You sound bitter."

"I'm just tired. So where do you want me to take you?"

Valentin leaned back against the wall and closed his eyes. "I can't think now. Can I have something to drink?"

"I'll get you some water. Do you want something to eat?"

He shook his head. "Just water for now. They didn't give me much...you know."

"It doesn't look like they gave you much of anything except grief." I poured water from the jug Halim had left earlier and placed the cup in Valentin's hands.

"You're angry."

"I am." I watched him hold the cup to his lips. His Adam's apple moved as he drank.

He drained the cup and held it out for more. "Anger will get you nowhere."

"I realize that. But it makes me feel better."

"I'm tired."

"I know. You should sleep."

"So should you."

"I will."

He nodded toward the chair. "On that?"

"If need be." I handed him another cup full of water.

Valentin swallowed it down and pushed the cup into my hand. "You are a bit soft-hearted really, aren't you?"

Only where you're concerned.

"I owe you."

He dropped his head back against the wall and closed his eyes once more. "You owe me nothing."

I opened my mouth to speak but he'd already drifted off again, his hands folded on his stomach. His chest rose and fell. I set the empty cup on the cabinet and left him so I could search for some food.

* * * *

When I returned, the room was in darkness. I lit a lamp and pulled the chair up to the bedside. Valentin had huddled back beneath the bedclothes once more. After a while, the day caught up with me. The chair bit into my shoulders, the hard wooden seat unyielding. I let my head drop and dozed, listening to the sounds of the city bedding down for the night, with the final call to prayer foremost. Valentin shifted restlessly under the covers, whimpering a little. The frown of a nightmare creased his brow. I took one of his hands and held it, hoping that the touch of another would calm him. He mumbled something in Russian, too slurred for me to make out. Then again in French with more urgency.

"Leave me, please." He shook off my hand, then swatted at something I couldn't see. "Oh Christ no!" Valentin thrashed at the bedclothes, fighting off an unseen enemy.

My pulse pounded in my ears.

Valentin flinched away from imaginary blows, curling up into a tight knot. The bedclothes tangled around his legs when he tried to kick them away. After a few moments, he stilled and whimpered, wrapping his arms over his head. I left the chair and sat on the bed, resting what I hoped was a reassuring hand on his shoulder. The bed shook with his silent, racking sobs.

"Valentin…it's all right. You're safe." I lay down beside him and gathered him up, holding him while wept in his nightmare.

He fell silent in time and huddled close, relaxing into my arms. I closed my eyes once more and fell asleep to the sound of his restful breathing.

* * * *

I woke before Valentin, feeling grubby for having slept through the night in my robes. I undressed, washed myself then put on a clean robe before heading downstairs in search of breakfast. I found Halim in the courtyard, taking slabs of flat bread from the clay oven.

"I have prepared breakfast," he told me. "There is fruit, bread and *chaka*. Shall I bring it up to the bedroom?"

"Thank you, yes. I think it's best I stay with the Captain and make sure he is all right."

Halim shook his head. "He is a very lucky man. Not many leave the Pit alive." He shuddered and placed a final piece of bread on top of the stack.

"Yes, he is lucky. I'm not sure he realizes that yet." I glanced at the open window upstairs. "Let's hope he gets better soon." I returned to the house and hurried up the stairs.

"Where were you?" Valentin regarded me with wild eyes.

"I was down in the courtyard talking with Halim. He is bringing breakfast shortly. Are you hungry?"

He hunched back against the wall, wrapping his arms around his knees. "I don't know…it's been so long… Who's

Halim?"

"He's a lad who works for Akmal. He's been sent here to look after us. It's all right. He's very trustworthy." This new Valentin scared me. All his arrogance was gone, replaced by this creature who cringed beneath the bedclothes. Everything inside me hurt at the sight of the wreckage he had become.

A soft rap on the door heralded Halim's arrival.

"Come in." I sat beside the bed and stole Valentin's hand, peeling it away from the sheet. "It's all right. Don't be scared."

His hand was cold and clammy. He tightened his fingers through mine and watched warily as Halim set the tray onto the chest that stood as a dresser. The aroma of fresh bread stole through the room. He carefully set the bowls and dishes down, bowed, then left.

Valentin released my hand and relaxed. "I think I could eat something."

I smiled at him. "I think you'd better."

He swung around and set his feet onto the floor. I winced at the sight of the sores on his legs. "I need to see to those today. If you don't mind."

Valentin glanced down. "What? Oh...those. Yes, it might not be a bad idea."

I stood up and held out my hand to help him to his feet. He tottered toward the food like an old man.

"Oh Jesus, I don't know where to start." He stared at the array of dishes.

"Slowly. Don't eat too much too fast. There's plenty of food in the house, you won't want for anything, whenever you want it."

He picked up an empty dish and placed a handful of cherries on it, followed by some melon and grapes, then retreated to the bed once more. He sat cross-legged on top of the rumpled bedclothes, evidently without care for his naked state. I helped myself to some bread, honey and fruit and sank onto my chair. I watched him pick carefully at the fruit, following my advice. He closed his eyes while he chewed, clearly savoring each mouthful until everything was gone.

"Do you want more?"

He nodded and handed me the empty dish. "Perhaps some of that bread with some honey?"

I rose to do his bidding. I poured a thin stream of honey on the bread and presented it to him.

"Thank you." He studied the repast. His bottom lip trembled and he sucked in a huge breath. "I can't remember..."

"Remember what?"

"What bread tastes like. What honey tastes like."

"Why don't you try and see?"

He tore a piece away and raised it to his lips. He took a tentative bite and chewed thoughtfully. It was like watching an infant trying something for the first time. Before long, the entire piece had disappeared. Valentin leaned against the wall and rubbed his distended stomach. "Very nice."

I took the empty plate. "Would you like some tea?"

"Please."

I poured him a cup of the thin green tea and took it to him. He downed it quickly, then rested once more. I watched the rise and fall of his chest. Pale, bruised skin stretched across a rib cage that was all too prominent.

"Let me dress those sores."

Valentin nodded weakly. "You won't hurt me, will you?"

I wanted to grab him by the shoulders and demand to know what they had done to him in that hellish place. Instead I found the bandages and salve that Akmal had provided. I poured water into the basin and carried it to the bed side. "Let me have a look."

He sighed, nodded and scooted down until he lay flat on the bed. I leaned over and carefully examined the sores, ignoring Valentin's tight little hisses if my touch was too firm. My examination complete, I dampened a cloth in the water then dabbed at the wounds as carefully as I could before applying the salve.

Valentin twitched at every touch.

"I'm sorry. I'm being gentle as I can. Don't worry, it'll soon be over." Once the salve was applied, I covered each sore with bandages until everyone was attended to. "There," I announced, "I'm done."

He nodded almost imperceptibly. "Thank you. You're being so patient and kind."

"It's the least I can do. We need to get you better. The sooner you recover, the sooner we can leave."

"Not yet though?"

"No, not yet. You are too weak." *And too damaged.* I wanted the old Valentin back, the one who owned the world and everything in it.

"I want to leave this place."

"I know." I patted his wasted leg and pulled the cover over his nudity. "Now you should rest."

"What about you? What will you do?"

"I'm not going to do much of anything. I shall sit here with you."

"You don't have to."

"I know. But I want to. You have been through a terrible ordeal. You're having nightmares. I'd rather stay and make sure that you're all right."

"You are too kind."

"It's in my best interests that you get well. I'm also anxious to get out of here."

He offered me the ghost of a smile. "It wouldn't have anything to do with getting rid of that beard would it?"

"That would be part of the reason, yes."

"Good. I prefer you without it. The damn thing hides your mouth. You have a very desirable mouth."

I took some hope from those words. Perhaps Valentin would return to me after all.

* * * *

"How is he?" Akmal sat cross-legged on the low divan in what passed for a sitting room in the lodging. The doors were open onto the courtyard, admitting a soft breeze.

"Weak, tired, and not himself. His stay in the Pit obviously affected more than his physical wellbeing. I'm beginning to believe that Stoddart and Connolly were probably desperate for death after all that time down there. Valentin was a strong soul before all of this. I hardly recognize him. He's broken. He has nightmares, sometimes forgets who or where he is, who I am. He keeps asking when we can leave."

"I'm sorry. He is one of the lucky ones. I know it doesn't seem like it at the moment, but he is. You will have to persevere, make him realize that the worst is over. That one day soon you can both ride away from this place."

"I know. It's hard. I am not a nurse and I am not a patient man when it comes to caring for others so intimately."

Akmal laughed. "I can imagine. You are not a man given to sitting still and waiting around. What are you doing with your time?"

"Reading the Koran. I might as well make myself even more familiar with it. No point in making a liar of myself. It passes the time."

"Excellent, perhaps I shall quiz you."

"Perhaps you will not."

"Don't worry, my friend. You will soon be gone from this place. You can hide in your house with your books and your fireplace and the rain."

For the briefest of moments I wished I was there, listening to the rain beating against the windows, seeing the clouds obscure the mountainsides. I could almost smell the burning peat and feel the draft swirling around my feet. "Anything is better than this infernal heat. I'm not born to it. It saps my strength and makes me want to sleep all the time."

"Why do you think our men folk spend most of their days sitting in the shade beside a tea house, gossiping and sipping tea? It's the best way to cope."

"I'd even welcome that."

The creak of floorboards announced Valentin's wakeful state. I glanced at the ceiling and waited.

"Gabriel?" His voice was reedy with the weary petulance of an invalid.

I stood. "Excuse me, I'd better go and see what he needs."

Akmal rose. "I should probably go anyway. I'll leave you to resume your duties as a nurse. I will come and see you tomorrow."

"Thank you. I keep hoping that each day will be a little better, that the old Valentin will return."

"I hope so, for your sake."

I hurried up the stairs and found Valentin cowering in a corner of the room, trembling and clawing at the floorboards.

"What's wrong?" I wanted to weep at the wreckage.

"I heard a strange voice. It scared me. Are they back for me?" He sounded like a frightened child.

"No, it's all right. It was Akmal. He brought some more supplies and wanted to know how you were doing. That's all." I sat on the floor beside him and eased him into my arms.

He curled up against me, clutching at my robe with a shaking hand. "Are you sure?"

"Very sure." I stroked his hair and brushed my lips over his forehead. "No harm will come to you while I'm here, I promise you."

He craned his neck to look at me. "You do?"

"Always." I stood and pulled him to his feet. "Why don't you come and sit out in the courtyard for a little while? The fresh air will do you good."

He leaned on me for a moment. "I'm not so sure."

"You can't hide in here forever."

Valentin rested his brow on my shoulder, eyes screwed shut. It seemed right to hold him, so I did. He trembled beneath my touch and when he spoke, his words were almost lost, muffled. "I know. When I was...when I was in…that…place, I longed for sunlight. I would've given anything to feel the sun on my face. Now…I don't know."

"You need to get used to leaving this room." I stroked his back, soothing him as if I was trying to calm a fractious horse. "We have to get out of this godforsaken place while we still can." Anxiety tugged at me. Every day spent trying to lie low in Bukhara was a risk I was tired of living with.

He pressed his forehead to mine. "I'll do it."

"Good. I'll ask Halim to serve our evening meal out there."

"All right."

I touched his cheek, feeling the stubble under my fingertips, then raised his head until I could touch his lips with my own.

Valentin rested his hands on my shoulders and parted his lips beneath mine. A soft moan rose unbidden from my throat. I wound my fingers through his sleep-tousled hair and deepened the kiss, wanting him to react.

He lifted his hands to my face, palms warm on my skin. Every touch cautious and gentle, as if we'd never been entangled on that bed. After a few minutes, Valentin pulled away and studied me in silence. Memories appeared to move across his face. His eyes darkened to the gray of a summer storm. "All right. You win, Gabriel. I'll sit in the courtyard with you but only because I'm afraid to be on my own."

I took his hand. "I won't leave you if you don't want me to."

"I was on my own for too long. I hated the darkness."

"It will pass. You'll get better. I promise."

"Are you sure?"

"Yes, I'm sure. I miss you, my friend. I miss the cocky bastard that you were."

He twitched his lips in a careful half-smile. "It's up to you to find him again for me."

"I intend to. Now, I suppose you'd better put some clothes on before you go downstairs. What will you wear?"

"Not native gear, I don't think I could…"

I sorted through the chest at the foot of the bed and produced a pair of trousers and a linen shirt. "Will these do?"

"Perfect." He took them from me.

I watched him dress, easing into trousers that were now too big for him. He left the shirt half-unbuttoned and rolled up the sleeves. "All right?"

"Absolutely." There were traces of the old Valentin there. "Come on, let's get some fresh air."

I led him down the stairs and into the courtyard. Hamir had set up a bench and low table in the shade, spreading a rug over the bench. Valentin sank onto the seat. I sat beside him and he edged closer until his shoulder rested against mine. We sat in silence with the music of the fountain and the distant murmur of the city. Valentin ran his hand through his hair and puffed his cheeks.

"Are you all right?" I rested my hand on his knee.

"I'm all right. It's nice to get out of that room."

He flinched when Hamil stepped into the courtyard bearing a tray with tea things and a plate of sweetmeats and pastries. I patted his leg in what I hoped was a reassuring gesture.

Hamil set the things on the low table then departed with a shy smile. I poured the tea and handed a cup to Valentin.

He sipped his drink quietly and stared at the fountain. Droplets of water glinted in the sunlight. A bird fluttered down from the roof and bathed itself in the shallow pool. I envied its ability to find a means of escaping the relentless heat. Valentin picked up a pastry and bit into it, sending a shower of almond scented crumbs onto his lap.

"Christ, this is good."

"Hamil is a good cook."

"Yes he is." He finished the cake and took another, which he devoured with evident relish before reaching for his tea. "I could eat all of these."

"Go ahead. You need feeding up."

87

Valentin plucked at the drooping waistband of his trousers. "I suppose I do." He sighed heavily. "I just want to go home. I'm tired and the thought of an interminable journey across the bloody desert and up the sodding Volga exhausts me."

"It's no more an appealing trek than mine back to Calcutta. With a rather unpleasant reception waiting for me." A black cloud settled over me. Even a plate full of pastries and Valentin's company couldn't dispel the sudden onset of gloom and apprehension at the prospect of the arduous trek. "I'm tempted to write in my resignation and head home."

Valentin patted my knee, then squeezed it. "Did you do something to anger your superiors? I've given it a lot of thought and I can't help thinking that someone in Calcutta doesn't like you."

I studied my hands. "I think you're probably right. There was something that happened..."

"I thought as much." He unfurled himself and stretched out on the bench, resting his head on my lap. "Tell me."

"There's not much to tell. A chap called Hoskins. He doesn't like the Irish. He hates them." I stroked Valentin's hair absently, finding comfort in the act.

He closed his eyes and wrapped one arm around my knees. "Is that it?"

"He has his favorite, a nephew. Nice enough chap but useless. Falls apart at the first hint of trouble. He nearly got me shot in Kabul, nearly got himself killed. I'm the one who saved his neck. Hoskins wasn't impressed. He's been trying to get the nephew promoted for ages and that little incident made his protégé look a bit pathetic. Somehow it was all my fault. He pushed heavily for me to be sent here."

Valentin rolled onto his back and stared up at me. "So you've fallen foul of something as petty as politics and prejudice. I'm sorry." He reached up and trailed his fingers along my cheek.

I caught his hand and held it, palm upward, to my lips.

"It's all right. If I leave this place in one piece and make it home, I'll be happy. That's all I want."

"What will you do when you return to Ireland?"

"Hide away in my cottage and spend my days beside the fire reading books and drinking whiskey. Perhaps I'll even write about my travels." The notion certainly had some appeal. "What about you?"

Valentin sighed. "The same as you. The *dacha* has great appeal right now. Especially in winter, when it's cut off from what passes for civilization up there. Nothing but peace and quiet and snow. As long as I have a full pantry and plenty of logs for the fire, I'd be a happy man."

"It seems we both have the same sort of future to look forward to."

"I hope so." He sat up once more and ran his hand through his hair. "Will you write to me?"

"Of course I will. I should hate to lose touch after...all of this."

He offered me a wry smile. "I should imagine your Hoskins would have an apoplectic fit if he knew, don't you think?"

I had a sudden vision of Hoskins in my mind's eye, his cheeks flushed beetroot red, watery blue eyes bulging as I casually told him I'd slept with my Russian counterpart. "It's almost worth the long ride back to Calcutta just to tell him that."

"It's not worth the risk, my friend."

"Risk? I think it's safe to say my future with the service is looking a bit grim. If I'm lucky, they'll give me a desk job somewhere." I faced Valentin. "What about you? What will you do?"

"Resign. I've had enough. I'll file my report, tell them to leave the Emir alone and that's it." He raked his fingers over his stubble. "Sad isn't it? Here we are, in the prime of our lives, your career is buggered and I'm too battle weary to carry on."

"What a dreary thought." I studied my teacup.

"It doesn't have to be that way, you know." Valentin edged closer. He trembled beside me. His chest rose as he drew in a deep breath.

"What do you mean?"

"Are you in any hurry to return to Calcutta? Do you even want to go back?"

"It's not a case of wanting to. I *have* to."

He raised an eyebrow. "Says who?"

"I'm duty bound to."

"It's a long journey back, anything can happen."

I stared at him. "What are you getting at?"

"What would happen if you rode in the other direction, if you never returned to Calcutta?"

"I should think, after a while, they may send someone to search for me. If they don't find me, they'd assume I was dead."

A half-smile tugged at his lips. "Would that be such a bad thing?"

"Being dead? I should say so. I may have reached the end of my career but I had no plans on dying any time soon."

"Calm down." He held his hands out palm up. "Please be patient. This is hard for me to say."

"It's even harder for me to listen to. I detest riddles."

Valentin chuckled. The sound had a nervous edge to it. "All right, I'll just say it." He took a deep breath. "Would you travel back to St Petersburg with me? I...I...I don't think I want to be on my own for a while. I think my nerve might've gone. Just see me home in one piece and you can travel home from there."

I considered his suggestion for a moment, the scenario raising more questions than answers. "So you think I should let Calcutta think I've perished, escort you back to St Petersburg, then sail home where I can spend the rest of my life hoping that no one notices that I am actually alive?"

"Would anyone notice? Don't you live in the middle of nowhere?"

"I'd have a hard time explaining to my brother why, after

he's received a letter informing him of my untimely demise, I've turned up alive and well on his doorstep. Plus, if I'm caught, I'd be in more than a little trouble for desertion."

Valentin sighed and studied his hands. "Never mind. It was just a thought."

"I'm flattered that you want to spend more time with me than is absolutely necessary, that you think I'm capable of getting you home in one piece. I'll give it some thought."

He rewarded me with a hopeful smile.

I tried to dismiss the foolish quickening of my pulse. My mind raced ahead, considering the possibilities. "Just give me some time."

"I promise. I will. Thank you." Valentin reached for another pastry. The change in his demeanor gave me hope that, regardless of where my thoughts took me, we could soon leave Bukhara.

Chapter Seven

I sat down with my journal beside the window. Behind me, Valentin slept, sprawled across the bed as if he owned it. There was little else to do in the crushing early afternoon heat. Hamil dozed on a bench in the courtyard, occasionally waving a languid hand at errant flies. The previous day's conversation meant that my mind kept me from rest. I had decisions to make. I wondered if the simple act of holding a pen in my hand would help, if writing down the options made the ultimate decision any clearer.

What was obvious to me was that Valentin was not in a state of mind to travel on his own. If I could deliver him to the Russian garrison at Fort Alexandrovsk, it would be something. It meant an arduous journey across the desert, risking bandit attacks, but with fit, healthy animals, it was possible.

The courtyard gate flew open with a discordant clang. The pen slipped from my fingers and Hamil leaped to his feet when Akmal hurried into the yard. "Gabriel!"

I stuck my head out of the open window. "I'm here."

"We must talk. Now." Akmal's tone suggested urgency.

I hurried down the stairs and met him in the doorway. "What's wrong?"

He grabbed my arm. "My friend, I think you must leave as soon as you can."

"What?" The words didn't quite register. "Why?"

"The Emir was asking questions. He wanted to know whether that Russian had left Bukhara yet. He thinks, if he hasn't, he needs to."

"He's not really ready to travel. He's only been free a

handful of days. He's still weak. He spends most of his time sleeping." I kept my voice low, mindful of the open window. "And…" I tapped my temple with my forefinger. "He's not right in the head. The whole ordeal has left him fearful of everything. He wants me to travel with him to St Petersburg. He doesn't feel comfortable traveling on his own."

Akmal sighed and shook his head. "Perhaps that would be best. What is clear is that you can't stay. If he finds out that he's been deceived…"

Leaden weight sank into my gut. A stream of curses, none of them polite, hovered at my lips. For Akmal's sake, I kept them to myself. "It looks like the decision has been taken from my hands. I've been considering taking him as far as the Russian garrison at Alexandrovsk. It looks like that's where I'll be going before I head to Calcutta."

"I'm sorry. It is not fair. But you must leave. If anyone should come looking for you, what shall I tell them?"

I sank onto a bench and stared at the Bukhara dust. A bird called out in the heavy afternoon silence. I took a leap into the dark.

"Tell them I left for Calcutta. Then you heard that I'd been set upon by bandits, one of whom was heard bragging in the bazaar. How they left my body for the vultures."

Akmal regarded me with wide eyes. "You want them to think you're dead?"

"Yes. I've had enough. If I return to Calcutta, I'll spend the rest of my working life in an office somewhere reading reports and writing more. Valentin asked me to take him to St Petersburg so I will. From there, I don't know. I shall have to write to my brother so it's not a complete shock to him when I turn up alive and well back in Ireland."

"Do what you must. I hope you don't get into trouble."

"I've spent the last ten years getting in and out of trouble. I'll get by. I doubt anyone will bother me. I've learnt how to hide myself."

"I hope so." Akmal patted my shoulder. "I'll arrange

for some supplies for your journey. I'll bring them by this evening. It might be best if you left in the morning, as soon as possible."

"Yes, you're right. We do need to get out of here." I rose, feeling like I'd aged by several hundred years. "I'd better tell Valentin."

"I'm sorry."

"It's all right. I'll be glad to be out of here. This is just the spur Valentin needs. If he's thinking of something else, he won't have time to brood over what's happened to him."

"I'll come back as soon as I can with your supplies." Akmal hurried back toward the gate.

Hamil wandered out of the kitchen. "The master has gone already?"

"I'm afraid so. And Master Yakolev and myself will be leaving tomorrow morning. Perhaps you could make some bread for us and put some food together. Food we can travel with."

The boy nodded. "Right away. I will also prepare a fine feast for your last meal here."

"Thank you." My appetite had just about disappeared but it was likely to be the last decent meal I'd have for some time. "That would be very nice."

I left him and headed for the stairs, wondering how best to break the news to Valentin.

He still slept, one arm flung carelessly behind his head while the other rested across his stomach. A flush colored his cheeks, hiding the pallor of his imprisonment. It was too bloody soon.

I sat on the edge of the bed and rested my hand on his thigh, feeling the warmth of him beneath my palm. I wasn't ready to say goodbye to him just yet.

"Gabriel?" Valentin's voice was little more than a rusty croak. "What's wrong?"

"I have some news." I swallowed, wishing there was time for diplomacy. "You won't like it."

He sat up. His hair stood in dense spikes.

94

I wanted to smooth them down. Instead, I withdrew my hand from his thigh and took a deep breath. "We have to leave. Akmal was here. The Emir has been asking questions. I think he wants to make absolutely sure that you're gone. We'll leave in the morning…early."

Valentin scratched at his stubble. "Tomorrow?"

"Yes."

"I'm not sure I can manage more than a few hours' riding a day. I certainly don't think I'm ready to travel on my own yet." He tightened his fingers around the bedclothes. "Christ, this is a bit brutal."

"You won't be on your own. I'll travel with you. I'd thought about taking you as far as Fort Alexandrovsk, but I may as well take you all the way to St Petersburg. I've told Akmal that if anyone comes looking for me, to tell them I'd been killed by bandits. I'll worry about what or how to get word to my brother later. Right now, the most important thing as that we both get out of Bukhara while we still can."

Valentin slumped against the wall. "You'll do that…for me?"

"If you can guarantee me safe passage once we reach Russia. I'd hate to be arrested for espionage."

"Don't worry. I'll vouch for you." He leaned forward, suddenly animated. "We can get travel papers sorted out at Alexandrovsk."

"Assuming we get there in one piece. It won't be an easy trek." It exhausted me thinking about it.

"We'll get there." He leaped out of bed. "I suppose we'd better get packed."

"Not a bad idea. I'll see to the horses. Akmal is bringing some supplies and Hamil is down in the kitchen cooking up a farewell feast. I suggest we take advantage of it because we won't be eating as well for a long time, I suspect."

Valentin struggled into his trousers, then reached for his shirt. "A grand send-off. Yes, we'll need it."

I left him to his packing and went to check on the horses.

* * * *

Akmal handed me the lead rein for the camel. "Safe travels, my friend."

I eyed the beast with some misgiving. The damn thing would slow us down but we needed it to carry enough supplies to see us across the desert. "Thank you." I shook Akmal's hand. "Thank you for everything." I swallowed at the lump in my throat, knowing it to be highly unlikely that I'd ever see him again.

His eyes were a bit too bright. "And you, my friend."

Valentin strode out of the stable, leading his horse and looking out of place in his everyday clothes. "Are we ready then?"

"Yes." I gathered up my reins. "We'd better get moving before it gets too hot. If it's still quiet, at least there's more chance that the right people will see us leave and tell the Emir."

He mounted his horse with far less grace than I remembered and slumped into the saddle. "All right then. The sooner we get out of here, the better."

Akmal looked at Valentin then stilled, the color drained from his cheeks. He seized my arm. "I need to have a word with you in private."

The urgency in his voice alarmed me. "Of course. What on earth is the matter?"

He pulled me back toward the house and stopped in the kitchen doorway. "I know him," he whispered, glancing past me toward Valentin who fiddled with his saddle, apparently in ignorance of our conversation.

"What do you mean?" I wondered if Akmal had lost in mind.

"I've seen him before."

"Of course you have. He came to your house to tell me about the execution."

"No, no...that's not where... It's been bothering me. There was something about him..." Akmal drew a deep breath. "Kabul. I saw him in Kabul, I'm sure of it. He was in one of the bazaars."

I stared at him for a moment, trying to absorb his words. "Are you sure?"

"Yes, I'm sure. I remember him now."

A lump of ice settled into my stomach. "I suppose it's possible." I didn't want to think about the implications.

"You be careful. Don't trust him. Please." He dug his fingers into my arm for emphasis.

"All right. I'll be careful. I hope that you're wrong." I wanted to be sick.

"So do I." Akmal let his hand fall away. He accompanied me back to my horse and held the reins while I climbed onto its back. He walked alongside to the gate where Hamil waited, openly weeping.

"Goodbye, masters. Safe journey."

"Thank you, Hamil. Work hard for your master. He'll take care of you."

He sniffed and nodded, still clutching the purse of coins I'd given him. "I will, sir."

Our little cavalcade stepped out onto the street. Morning shadows stretched across the narrow way. The aroma of baking bread drifted in the cool breeze. The call to prayer sounded from a distant minaret. For all the illusion of peace, there was a rottenness at Bukhara's heart and I was glad to be riding away from it. I glanced back past the camel, past Valentin and waved to Akmal, who stood with Hamil outside the house. Part of me would remain there forever.

* * * *

"That's that then." Valentin sighed when we rode through the city gates and left the shadow of the walls behind us.

I stared north at the vast, arid stretch of desert beyond the green ribbon of fields. The cloudless sky held nothing but heat even at such an early hour. In spite of everything, including what Akmal had just told me. I shared Valentin's relief. "I'm glad to be away from the place." I nudged my horse out of his sleepy amble. "And the farther away we get, the better."

The camel bawled in protest and fell into a shambling stride behind me. Valentin brought his horse alongside mine. We turned to the northwest, away from the Silk Road and onto another trade route. I'd checked our firearms the night before, and made sure they were operable. Akmal had also managed to 'acquire' a pair of serviceable Brunswick rifles which were strapped, conspicuously displayed, to our saddles. I hoped it would be enough to deter any potential bandits. One nervous Irish man and a half-sick Russian didn't really present much of an opposition to troublemakers.

* * * *

The oasis was too small to accommodate more than a couple of travelers, a fact for which I was grateful. Valentin slumped in his saddle, his delight at leaving Bukhara in the dust long gone by late afternoon.

"This looks as good a place as any," I said, reining my horse to a halt beneath a tree.

"It's fine." Valentin slid from the saddle and drew the reins over his gelding's head. "It's cooler, it's quiet and there's water."

I dismounted and set about tethering the camel. It spat in protest, snaking its head toward me. White foam flecked its lips and it regarded me with a baleful eye when I nudged it behind one knee. It dropped to its knees with a roar but remained still.

"Somebody doesn't like you." Valentin set his saddle on the ground.

"If you think you can do better, you're more than welcome to take care of the wretched beast."

"No, it looks like you're doing a splendid job. I'll see to your horse, if you like."

"Thank you." I tied the lead rope around the tree trunk and began the tiresome chore of unburdening the beast and getting our camp ready for the night. By the time I'd finished, Valentin had collected water from the well and had a small fire going.

I dug my battered old basin from the baggage and filled it with water.

"What are you doing?"

"Getting rid of this damned beard."

"You are? I don't blame you. I think I hate it as much as you do."

"Why's that?" I stropped my razor. "You don't have to wear the bloody thing."

"It makes you look like an Imam and there's part of me that's disgusted with myself for wanting to fuck you when you look like that. I'm sure I shall burn in hell."

"I think we're both already destined for hell for our preferences." I propped my small bit of mirror against the basin and tilted it to the right angle. "I haven't set foot in a confessional since the first time I…well, you know."

"I know. I stopped feeling guilty a long time ago."

I scraped the blade across my cheek and concentrated on shaving, aware that Valentin watched every careful sweep of the razor until I'd finished. My chin felt exposed and stung when the breeze touched it.

"Christ." Valentin's voice escaped in a hoarse whisper. "If I wasn't so tired I'd—"

"You'd keep your hands off me." I glared at him. "Bukhara was…different. We can't fuck our way to St Petersburg."

"Why not? We need to pass the time somehow, especially when we're on the river."

I pushed the temptation aside. "I'm not generally given to sleeping with people I don't really know." I realized how little I knew him. I pushed thoughts of what he might've done in Kabul to the back of my mind. This was not the time.

"That didn't stop you before."

99

"That was different."

"So you only slept with me because of what I could do for you."

I took a deep breath. "That was the agreement."

"You certainly seemed to enjoy it, considering it was nothing more than business." Petulance colored his tone.

"I did...very much. I'd be lying if I said I didn't want to repeat the experience. I do."

"Then what's stopping you?"

"Call it old fashioned Catholic guilt and the fact that I think we should worry about getting the hell away from this place before we think about hopping into bed together again."

He sighed, a trifle theatrically. "When did you acquire a conscience?"

"It's more a case of self-preservation. Let's get to Alexandrovsk and then I'll reconsider."

"You do like to think things over, don't you?" His eyes brightened a little.

"Yes. I tend to get into trouble if I rush into things."

"You think I'll get you into trouble?"

I think you'll break my heart.

"I'd say there's every possibility." He didn't need to know the truth.

"Then I shall have to learn patience." He leaned across the space between us and trailed his fingers down my cheek. "Perhaps you should've kept the beard. Then I'd be less tempted."

I rose, walked to the nearest tree then poured the shaving water into the dry soil. "I can always let it grow back."

"No, I'll try and restrain myself. I haven't the energy anyway." He flopped back onto his bedroll and closed his eyes. "I'm already exhausted."

"Then rest. I'll take care of things. I'll wake you when it's time to eat."

"Thank you." He folded his arms behind his head and, within moments, his deep, even breathing told me he was already asleep.

"If I never see desert again, it will be too soon." Valentin spurred his horse into a trot. "I hate this fucking place."

I glanced behind at the empty road. A vague prickling at the back of my neck had plagued me for two days. After several years of solitary travel I'd learnt to trust that niggling feeling. "So do I." I touched the warm butt of the rifle to reassure myself of its presence.

The landscape ahead was free of landmarks, and very little cover. If my gut instinct was right, we'd need it. "Are you up to traveling a little faster?" I wound the camel's rope around my hand and tugged.

"I think so. Why?"

"We may have a problem. Make sure you can grab your rifle if you need to."

Valentin craned his neck to look back. "I don't see anything."

"Someone's there. Or, more worryingly, some people."

"Fuck." He dug his heels into his horse's flanks. It squealed and lunged forward, ears pinned back.

I rode behind, willing the camel to hurry. It broke into an easy lope alongside and the rope went comfortably slack. I'm sure if I dropped the rope, it would've followed but it was hardly the time to put my trust in the beast to the test.

We raced along the road, leaving dust in our wake, which made it virtually impossible to see if our pursuers had taken up the chase or not. All that mattered was that we could see where we were going.

"Up there." Valentin pointed toward a crumbling mud wall which rose out of the desert. "That'll have to do."

I nodded and reined my horse in that direction, following in Valentin's wake.

He drew his gelding to a stuttering halt and jumped to the ground. I followed, my progress made more awkward by the camel. Valentin grabbed my horse's reins and led it around to the other side of the ruin while I tugged at the suddenly reluctant camel. It roared and nearly sat back on its haunches before Valentin gave it a swift kick. Finally, it lurched forward and followed me. When we reached the other side of the wall, I nudged it behind the knee and it obligingly dropped to the ground with a low, liquid grumble. The wall was all of five feet high. Shelter enough, another lower wall ran at a one hundred and eighty degree angle, which ended in a pile of stones. It was more than I could've hoped for. Only the lack of shade presented a problem in the relentless July heat.

Valentin checked his rifle and set his musket on the ground beside him. I peered over the wall.

"Anything?"

"Not yet. At least we have a little time." I passed him a canteen of water. "You'll need this."

He took a sip, then wiped his mouth. "I hope the bastards don't keep us waiting. I hate the waiting."

I rested my rifle on the wall and leaned against the warm stone. "So do I. Dare I ask if you're a decent shot?"

He grinned. "One of the best in my regiment. You?"

"Passable."

"That's not very comforting."

"I'll get by. Shall we have a competition? The person who shoots the least has to make dinner."

"Challenge accepted." He held his hand out.

I shook it. Reluctant to let go. The fearful wreck seemed to have disappeared for the moment. The old Valentin had returned, eyes alight with the thrill of facing danger.

Valentin edged closer until his shoulder rested against mine. His presence quelled the churning in my gut. I suddenly felt able to take on an entire army if I had to.

"We'll be fine."

"If you say so."

He brushed his lips over mine for the briefest of moments. Desire almost overcame my apprehension. I wanted to grab him and take him there and then. Valentin stepped back and turned toward the road. Several specks materialized in the distance, their presence heralded by a drift of dust.

I loaded gunpowder and a ball into the barrel, rested the rifle on the wall and waited for our visitors to come within range.

Valentin stood beside me, finger already on the trigger as he readied his aim. The bandits drew closer.

Five hundred yards.

Four hundred yards.

"Ready?" Valentin shouldered his rifle and squinted, creases fan-tailing away from the corner of his eyes.

"Yes." I raised the gun and, when I judged the first of the horsemen to be within three hundred yards, took aim, winced at the recoil then ducked to avoid the returning gunfire.

"You missed." Valentin pulled his trigger.

A distant yelp and a horse reeling around told me that his shot had found its mark. "Well done."

He grinned and loaded another round while I made ready to fire my second.

This time my shot found its target. Another bandit tumbled to the dirt.

"Bugger." Valentin's second went wide.

Puffs of dust and the mosquito drone of bullets drove us to seek cover behind the wall. I hurriedly loaded my third as the relentless tattoo of hoof beats grew louder. "How many left?"

Valentin popped his head above our makeshift parapet then dove for cover. "Three."

I took aim and squeezed the trigger. The recoil bit into my shoulder. I'd feel that in the morning, if we survived. My intended target screeched and tumbled from his horse. I found grim satisfaction in the moment, knowing that if the bugger had survived, I'd be the one being killed.

"Two left." Valentin fired his third round off quickly then scrambled to the ground when one of our attackers fired back. "Persistent bastards."

"Only two?" I peered over the wall. "There's only one left now." I fired at the sod. My shot went wide, feathering the dust somewhere to the right of the horseman. He hauled his animal to a sliding stop and let loose a stream of colorful curses, before wheeling around and charging past the bodies of his fallen comrades.

"Shall we let him go?" Valentin poured more powder into his barrel, tamped it down and dropped the ball in.

"So he can get help? No."

"Right then." He lifted the rifle, braced himself and fired. The survivor dropped to the ground like a sack of potatoes, leaving his horse to chase after its comrades. "I believe it's your turn to make dinner."

I stared at the carnage. Five men felled by a handful of shots. I told myself that if we hadn't killed them, we'd have been the ones lying dead beneath the burning July sun. "What do we do with the bodies?"

Valentin spat into the dust. "Leave the bastards. They can serve as a warning." He slung his rifle over his shoulder and strode toward his waiting horse. "They would've cut our throats given half a chance."

I retrieved the camel and my horse. Valentin had already remounted and turned his horse toward the road. I secured my rifle and clambered into the saddle. I didn't look back as we rode away. It wasn't the first time I'd killed anyone, but it never got any easier to live with.

* * * *

"So what are you making for my dinner?" Valentin sank down on his bedroll and sat cross-legged, facing me.

I poured rice into the boiling water. "What we've eaten every night since leaving Bukhara."

"Rice."

"Your enthusiasm for the meal is less than encouraging. I'll add some currants and spice, will that help?"

He shrugged. "It might, but what would help more would be a nice bit of lamb or mutton."

I stared past him at the open expanse of desert beyond the tiny oasis we'd camped in. "If you can find one in this godforsaken place, then I could add some mutton."

"All right, spare me your wit." Valentin sighed and stared glumly at the bubbling pot. "I will never eat rice again. When I get home, I'm going to have a feast made up of everything I've missed."

I dropped a pinch of spice mix into the rice, along with a handful of dried fruit. "What kind of things do you miss?"

He rested his elbows on his knees and gazed into the pale flames. "A simple consommé to start, then perhaps a plate of oysters, then poulet Marengo, with all the vegetables I can eat and to finish, a charlotte russe or a plate of fruit and cheese, all washed down with a bottle of two of excellent French wine. Or, even better, a big bowl of *shchi*. That's my favorite when I'm at the *dacha*. What about you?"

"Roast lamb, or roast beef. It doesn't matter which. A glass or two of claret. I'd be very happy with that. I'd be happy with a loaf of bread and a bit of cheese." I thought of sitting beside the fire, legs stretched across the hearthrug to take advantage of the warmth while rain hurled itself against the windows. The lamps would be lit to ward off the wintry gloom and the curtains would stir in the draft, but it wouldn't matter. "And rain, I miss rain."

"Snow. Lots of snow. I miss that silence and that stillness."

"Sounds…peaceful."

"It is. That's why I like the *dacha*. No one would dare venture there in the winter. When the family visit, it's only for a week or two in the summer. It drives my mother mad that I refuse to live in St Petersburg." He sighed again. "She doesn't think I stand a chance of finding a wife if I shut myself away in the country all year round."

"Thank heavens my parents have never really given me grief about that. As long as my sister-in-law continues to produce babies, I'll be left in peace. It's one of the advantages of being the younger son."

"I think my brother suspects that I'm not interested in women. He usually tells my mother to drop the subject." Valentin shrugged. "It's not like it matters. My brother was looking for someone to marry. He probably has by now. Another family occasion I was able to avoid."

I stirred the rice and placed the lid on the pot. "I think I could endure a family occasion if it meant being far away from this wretched bloody place."

"I suppose I could too. I'll just be happy to set foot on Russian soil again."

"How long have you been away?"

Valentin shifted, raising his knees and wrapping his arms around his legs, as if he was trying to curl up into himself. "I'm not entirely sure. Two years? Yes, that sounds about right. How about you?"

"Ten." Homesickness flared and twisted in my gut. I closed my eyes and remembered green grass and the constant murmur of the waves creeping onto the crescent of sand beyond my cottage. For a moment I could almost feel the damp wind brushing my cheeks. Whatever shreds of guilt I felt for walking away from my job faded, overwhelmed by my longing to leave the game.

"You look as homesick as I feel." Valentin's voice was gentle. He reached across and touched my cheek. "Don't worry, we'll be away from here soon."

"Thanks." I tried not to think of the long journey to get there, the days we had left in the desert, the long trip along the Volga...Ireland seemed to belong to another realm, one that existed only in my imagination.

I just wanted to go home.

Chapter Eight

Valentin reined his horse to a stuttering halt and stared ahead. "We're not far now, by my reckoning."

I gazed at the flat, featureless landscape. "How can you possibly tell?" Thirty-three days traveling had made me testy and Valentin waking me every night with his screams of terror left me exhausted.

"That little clump of trees over there, that's a landmark I recognize."

"So how far?"

"About a day's ride."

"Thank Christ for that." I fancied the breeze that blew from the west carried the scent of the sea with it, a flat, salty tang. I could almost hear the gulls.

He smiled. "Anyone would think you were anxious to be away from here."

I glared at him.

"Don't worry. Life will soon get a lot easier."

"Good. As long as I never have to eat another bowl of rice, I'll be fine."

Valentin nudged his horse forward and mine fell in alongside while the camel trotted serenely behind us. It had finally decided we were worthy of its company and no longer needed to be led. I sat deeply in the saddle and let my mind drift. It was the only way to forget the monotony. Four months on a steamboat slowly churning its way up the Volga would be paradise.

"*Merde!*" Valentin pulled his horse up once more and reached for his rifle.

"What?" I snapped out of my meandering in time to see a

cloud of dust to the west of us.

"Christ, I wish people would just leave us alone. How many times is this now?"

"I think this is the third or fourth." I glanced around, searching for cover. We were getting adept at fighting off the bandits. I tried not to think of the trail of dead men we'd left behind us — all foolish enough to think we were an easy target.

"Over there, that little depression in the ground. That'll have to do." Valentin urged his horse forward then jumped off. "It's bloody useless."

"We'd better shoot the bastards before they start shooting at us then." I jumped down from my horse. "I don't want to lose our animals after all this time."

Valentin had already dropped to his stomach in the shallow ditch. "We won't."

The camel dropped to its knees with a bubbling roar of protest. I grabbed my rifle and scrambled into the hollow, scraping my bare elbows on the rocky ground as I settled in beside Valentin. "Can you see how many?"

"Looks like three to me. All waving their guns in the air. Fools." He spat into the dust and glared down the barrel of his gun.

I followed the direction of his gaze and watched them approach, riding scrappy, half-starved horses, yelling their threats and insults. I'd lost all patience with the place and the people. I loaded the rifle and prepared to fire.

"Should be easy pickings." Valentin observed. "They're almost too stupid to shoot."

"They're annoying me." I took aim at the first one, conspicuous in his light robes. He held his pistol out before him, ready to take a shot. The trigger yielded to the pressure of my finger. I braced for the recoil, wincing as the butt bit into my shoulder. The horseman fell without a whimper, hitting the ground already dead.

"Excellent shot. My turn next." Valentin fired then ducked as the first of the bullets spat into the dirt around us.

Another bandit slumped from his saddle. His horse squealed and ground to a halt. The surviving horseman kept riding toward us, shouting obscenities and firing. I had a moment or two to admire his horsemanship before I raised my gun and took aim, hoping to nail him before he got in another shot.

A burning knife skewered my left shoulder, flinging me face first into the dust.

Valentin swore, fired his rifle, then flung it to the ground. "Gabriel?"

"I'm still here. What happened?"

"Bastard, bastard, bastard." His voice shook. I couldn't tell whether it was with fury or fear.

"Shouldn't you be shooting something?"

"I did. I got him, right between the eyes. Now let me look at you."

"Just tell me what happened." I rolled onto my side.

"You've been shot."

"I did wonder. It's beginning to hurt a bit."

"Can you sit up?"

"Of course I can." I pulled myself out of the dirt and sat up slowly, then closed my eyes to stop the world spinning. Fire coursed through my skin, digging deeper.

Valentin was pale. "I'm going to take your shirt off."

I raised an eyebrow. "This is hardly the —"

"Not the time for jokes, Gabriel." He fumbled with my buttons, fingers shaking.

I curled my hand around his wrist. "It's all right. I'm awake aren't I? I'm alive. It's only my shoulder." I tried to push the pain and dizziness away, figuring if I made light of it, it would stop hurting.

He dropped his head until his forehead rested against mine. "I'm sorry. It just scares me seeing you hurt."

I tried to lift my hand to tackle my shirt buttons. A freshet of pain scorched down my arm. I bit my lip.

Valentin took a deep breath. "Don't. I'll do it." He tackled my shirt once more, with calmer fingers, keeping his brow pressed to mine. In different circumstances, it might have been an erotic moment, leading to much better things. With the last button addressed, Valentin eased my shirt back. I couldn't help wincing when the fabric clung stubbornly to the site of the wound.

"Pour some water on it, that should help unstick the bloody thing," I told him.

He scrambled across the ditch and pulled the water bottle from his saddle.

The water stung, reigniting the flames. Valentin set the bottle down and pulled carefully. My eyes watered. I curled my good hand into a fist and concentrated on the bite of my fingernails into my skin rather than the waves of agony from my shoulder.

"Right, straighten your arms."

I complied, the left arm more cautiously than the right.

"I'm going to take this off now."

"All right. I'm ready."

Valentin tugged lightly on the fabric, it was almost a relief when he tossed the shirt to one side. "I'm going to pour more water on it."

"Fine." I braced myself for more pain.

The water burnt like acid. A gasp escaped my lips.

"Oh God, I'm sorry." Valentin whispered. "I just need to see if I can find the ball and get it out."

Oh Christ.

"Can you?"

He touched my shoulder, leaned close and kissed the back of my neck. "I can see it. It must've ricocheted off something before it hit you, it hasn't gone very deep, thank Christ."

"So you can get it out?"

"Do you have any alcohol?"

"The flask in my saddle bag. There's some whiskey left."

"Good, because you're going to need it." Valentin hurried over to my horse, who stood dozing in the hot sun, and found the flask. He returned and held it out to me. "Drink,

drink as much as you can stand. I'm going to set up some shade. We can't sit out in the sun like this."

"I hadn't even thought about it." The pain in my shoulder consumed me. The musket ball an alien presence, pressing into my flesh.

He returned to the camel, pulling bits and pieces from the carefully packed baggage until the ground was scattered with bags, boxes, bottles. Finally, he produced the poles and square of canvas we hadn't needed to use on our journey.

I wrapped my good arm around my knees and watched him hastily assemble the crude shade and erect it by driving the poles firmly into the soil. Then he unfurled my bed roll and spread it out.

"How's that?"

"Fine."

Valentin lifted me cautiously and helped me to the shade. In spite of the heat of the day, the air felt slightly cooler beneath the musty smelling canopy. I flopped face down onto the bed roll.

"Nope, not yet. Sit up."

I complied, wincing.

"Here, drink as much of this as you can stand." He shoved the warm flask into my hand.

I took a deep breath and raised the flask to my lips while Valentin scrabbled about gathering bits of dried grass and brush and made a pile.

"What are you doing?"

"I need a fire. Once I've got the bullet out, I'll need to cauterize the wound."

I gulped another mouthful of whiskey, ignoring the embers settling into my gut. Then I drank more, telling myself it was just odd tasting water, vowing never to drink like that again. A great, languid wave settled over me. I handed the flask to Valentin and shook my head slowly. "That's it. I can't drink anymore."

"Are you sure?" Doubt colored his voice.

"If I drink anymore, I'll be sick. Everything is spinning."

"All right." He pocketed the flask and eased me back down onto the bedding. "You'd better take this." He passed me a knotted handkerchief. "Stick it in your mouth. If and when I hurt you, bite down on the knot."

I complied, then rested my head on my good arm.

Valentin pulled a small hunting knife from its leather sheath. I closed my eyes, not wanting to see any more.

"Forgive me," he whispered before brushing his lips over my good shoulder. "I'll try to make this as quick as possible. Do you trust me?"

I nodded. I tried not to think of Kabul, reasoning that if he'd wanted me dead he would've killed me long before that moment.

He straddled my hips, his weight a welcome distraction. "All right, here goes."

I closed my eyes and bit down on the grimy fabric as the blade touched my skin.

"Jesus." Valentin muttered.

Something bit me, something with fangs rimmed with fire. I yelled then screamed when the pain ripped through my body, radiating out from the bitter sting of the knife.

"I'm sorry, so sorry. Please forgive me."

The agony had reduced me to a speechless, gibbering fool. I clamped down hard on the handkerchief and fought the urge to throw Valentin off me, especially when he dug in once more. I felt droplets of his sweat trickle down my back.

"Nearly there. Hold on, please."

I clawed at the soil and braced myself for the onslaught, the next merciless wave of pain. I wasn't disappointed. This one swept over me like a storm. I screamed then the world tumbled into a welcome darkness.

* * * *

I woke to the soft cool breeze of nightfall. The pain in my shoulder had reduced to a thudding, nagging ache. The gentle snuffle of horses filled the silence along with the crackle of a fire, which cast a flickering light on the canopy.

"Gabriel?" Valentin trailed his knuckles over my cheek. "Are you all right?"

I shifted onto my side to see him more clearly, ignoring the twinge. "I think so."

He ducked his head, captured my chin with his hand and kissed me. "I'm sorry I hurt you. I didn't mean to."

"You had no choice. Did you get it out?"

Valentin grinned then shoved his hand into his pocket. He held the offending object between thumb and forefinger. "I did. Do you want to keep it?"

"No I bloody don't."

He shoved it back into his pocket. "Then I will. A little memento."

I struggled into a sitting position. "You're mad."

"Yes, I probably am. Several weeks in the Pit of Bukhara will do that to a man." He lifted my hand to his cheek and held it there. "You've kept me reasonably sane. I could not have managed this journey alone and you are the one who has paid the bigger price. Please forgive me."

"Did you shoot me?"

"No, of course I didn't."

"Then there's nothing to forgive. You got the bullet out, didn't you? I'm still alive."

"I wouldn't blame you if you wanted to turn around and head for Calcutta." He turned his head and touched my palm with his lips.

I shivered, and not from the vague chill of the evening breeze. "It's a bit late for that now. I don't want to. Not now. Not ever." My head ached from the raw whiskey. My shoulder throbbed, reminding me that the wound was altogether too recent.

"Are you all right?"

"I don't think so. It still hurts a bit, you know."

"Then you should sleep. Hopefully we can get to Alexandrovsk tomorrow and have the garrison doctor look at you."

"I'd like to sleep."

Valentin relinquished my hand and let me lie down. He spread his bedroll out beside mine, threw sand on the fire then settled next to me in the darkness. "Then sleep. I'll be here if you need me."

"Thank you." I rolled onto my side, trying to find the most comfortable position.

Valentin wrapped himself around me. "You can't roll over and hurt yourself this way." His breath was warm on my skin.

I settled into his arms, tired and wanting to retreat from the discomfort. "It's nice."

"Hmmmm, yes it is." He rested his chin on the top of my head.

I closed my eyes and drifted into sleep.

Chapter Nine

I clung to the pommel and tried not to let dizziness get the better of me. Everything ached and every part of me burned. Sweat stung my eyes. My fingers slipped over the reins. I wanted to sleep. I *needed* to sleep. Instead, I just slumped into the saddle and tried to find a comfortable position, shrinking away from the heat, even though it was inside me. I slid into a fevered dream, nonsensical and horrible, where the Emir shoved Valentin from the top of the minaret and bandits cheered his demise.

"Gabriel?" Valentin grabbed my arm.

"What?"

"Are you all right?"

I forced myself to open my eyes. "No. I don't feel all that well."

He reined his horse close to mine, leaned over and ran his hand down my neck. "You have a fever."

"Yes."

My horse slowed and stopped.

"We haven't far to go. Can you smell the sea?"

I lifted my chin and inhaled. Yes, it was there, that familiar smell. I fancied I could hear the plaintive cries of gulls, but that could've been wishful thinking. "I think so."

Valentin jumped down and eased me gently from the saddle. "I think it might be best if you ride with me. It's not far, my horse can take us both. We can get there quicker and you can see the doctor."

"That might be a good idea. I'm not sure I can stay upright in the saddle for much longer."

"I can see that." He guided my foot into the stirrup and

gave me a nudge.

I hauled myself into the saddle and waited while he climbed up behind me and took the reins in one hand, while he led my horse with the other. "Lean back against me. Try to rest."

"So hot…"

"I know. Not long now. Then you can rest."

"In a proper bed?"

"I'm not sure about that. But it will be better than sleeping on the ground."

I slumped against him, grateful to let him take the weight. His breath was warm on my cheek. I almost forgot about how ill I felt. How everything ached. Valentin's closeness was a balm that almost held the fever demons at bay. He nudged the horse into a quicker walk and it eased into a gentle rocking motion that soon had me drifting into sleep.

* * * *

"Gabriel." Valentin's whisper against my skin pulled me from my turbulent dreams. "Wake up."

I kept my eyes closed. It seemed too much of an effort to open them. "Why?"

"We've made it…thank Christ."

"Where?"

"Alexandrovsk."

Was that a kiss he left on my cheek? A fleeting warm touch.

I will never get to the depths of you, Valentin.

I forced my eyes open in time to see a well-beaten track stretching ahead of us toward a fort. The gates were open and a sentry sat on a stool at the threshold, watching our approach with mild interest. He didn't even raise his gun when Valentin slowed the horse and our ragged cavalcade halted before the walls. In my half-doze, it was hard to follow the exchange, all in French. But the end result was that the guard waved us through without argument and

116

called to someone inside.

"He's asked someone to get the doctor." Valentin reined his horse in then ran one hand over my brow. "How do you feel?"

"Awful...too hot."

"I can feel it. Don't worry. The doctor will help you." He slid from the horse's back and helped me to the ground. I leaned heavily against him, apparently incapable of putting one foot in front of the other without assistance. Someone, another soldier perhaps, took the horses and the camel and led them away, followed by another stream of French from Valentin.

I didn't really care. "I think I need to lie down." My throat was constricted by a tight band of pain.

"It's all right," Valentin tightened his arm around my waist. "Here comes the doctor."

I glanced up in time to see an elderly gentleman hurrying across the dusty square toward us.

"Ah, gentlemen. Sorry to keep you waiting."

I could just about understand his French, colored as it was with an overlay of Russian accent.

"What's wrong?"

"He was shot yesterday, ricochet. I managed to get the ball out, but now he's running a fever and he's not well. He's tired and restless in his sleep."

"Bring him through to the infirmary and I'll take a look at the wound. Did you cauterize it?"

"Yes." Valentin helped me toward a portico and, beneath that, through a doorway. The room was cool and dark, and felt like heaven after a month's journey over open desert.

"Over there, that bed in the corner."

I let Valentin guide me toward the bed. I stood as quietly as a child while he unfastened my shirt and removed it with care. Then, without being asked, I flopped face down onto the thin mattress. It was soft as a cloud after the weeks of sleeping on hard ground or on cots in roadside inns.

"Let's have a look then." The doctor's voice was bright

with good cheer. "What's your name, son?"

"Gabriel." I could just about manage that.

"How do you feel?" He removed Valentin's makeshift bandage.

"Hot and tired and sick." I just wanted to sleep.

"Hmmmm..."

I yelped when the doctor prodded at my back.

"It's infected." He sighed and rose. "I have some tincture of silver nitrate that might help. Other than that, we shall have to hope for the best. Don't move."

I smothered a yawn. "I won't."

Valentin sat down on the adjacent bed. "He doesn't exactly fill me with confidence," he whispered.

"I just need to sleep."

He reached over and brushed my cheek with the back of his hand. "I'll stay with you."

"I don't think that would be a good idea, do you? You're probably going to have to explain to someone why you've brought me here. The last thing you need is people wondering why you're sleeping in an infirmary next to an Englishman."

The doctor returned, carrying a bowl of water, cloths and a bottle. He set the bowl on the small cabinet beside the bed. "I'm sorry, this will hurt."

"I expect it will. It can't hurt any more than it did yesterday." I curled my fingers into the thin sheet and waited.

"You haven't done a bad job, Captain Yakolev. I couldn't have done much better myself." The doctor dampened a cloth, wrung it out, then dabbed at the wound. Raw pain swept through me. I turned my head toward Valentin who sat, knuckles whitened, on the very edge of the other bed.

"You'll be all right," he mouthed.

It certainly didn't feel that way when a thousand flaming needles pierced my skin. I shoved the linen into my mouth and bit down while the doctor applied the tincture. After several endless moments of searing agony, he leaned back.

"There. Hopefully that will help. Now I'll get you some morphine. You need to rest. The more you can rest, the better chance you have of fighting the infection."

I nodded, pain having stolen my words.

His knees creaked when he rose. His footsteps receded into a chorus of echoes. I was already going, drifting into darkness.

"I had best go and explain things to the garrison commander." Valentin's voice was lost in that darkness. "I'll be back."

"Mmmmph…" I remembered nothing more.

* * * *

I woke to the touch of a cool breeze floating through an open window. A single lamp flickered in the welcome draft. The heavy silence of night beyond the window was broken by the occasional call of a bird and the soft murmur of waves. My skin was damp, made cold by the moving air. I shivered and reached for my bedclothes, pulling them up with an aching arm.

"Let me." Valentin appeared at my bedside. He placed the thin sheet around my shoulders. "How are you feeling?"

I considered my answer for several moments. "Sore, drained."

"I'm not surprised. You've been fighting the fever for a couple of days." He placed his hand on my forehead. "And now it's gone."

"What are you doing here?"

"Giving the good doctor a rest. He's been looking after you during the day and I've been caring for you at nights." He moved his hand to my face, cupping my cheek. "It's good to see you looking better. Would you like some water?"

"Please." I struggled into a sitting position and tried to ignore the stabbing at my shoulder.

"Here, let me help you." Valentin slid his arm around my waist, propped the pillow against the wall, and eased me

119

upright. Then he leaned forward and kissed my forehead. "I've missed you."

I managed a smile and touched his face, feeling the roughness of a day or two's growth of whiskers beneath my fingertips. "Stop feeling guilty. It could've been much worse."

He laughed softly. "How well you know me."

"We've spent the better part of two months in each other's company. Of course I know you…in some ways."

Valentin handed me a tin mug. "Here you go. Drink this."

I sipped the brackish water carefully, letting it trickle down my parched, aching throat until I'd emptied the cup. "Thank you."

"Do you want more?"

"No, that's enough for now." I rested against the pillow. "I don't want to make myself sick."

"I don't want you to make yourself sick." Valentine perched on the side of my bed and held my hands between his. "There's a supply boat arriving tomorrow. We can leave when it sails. It'll take us to Astrakhan and we can pick up a steamboat from there. Do you think you're up to it?"

"I'll make sure I am. I don't want to stay in this bloody desert any longer than I have to."

"I've sorted out your travel documents. The commanding officer here is most obliging, since I've given him some useful information about our mutual 'friend', the Emir."

"Good. What did you tell them about me?"

"That you had saved me from the Pit. That was enough. You are a hero now. He's writing a letter of commendation to the Tsar."

I stared at him. "How do I merit that? Are you more important than you've made yourself out to be?"

Valentin grinned, raised my hand to his lips and kissed my knuckles. "I have my…supporters."

"Must you be so oblique?"

"I'm just the same as you. I worked for my government, as you did. Now I'm done and so are you. We've played our games."

"Yes," I replied, too tired to say much else, "Yes we have."

Chapter Ten

I leaned on the boat's railings and stared at the muddy bank of the Volga. A cool wind moved through the reeds, marked by a spreading silver wave. Gulls wheeled overhead, crying out in the late summer sky.

Valentin stood beside me, his shoulder touching mine. The breeze moved through his hair and his eyes took on the blue-gray of the quiet water. "We're finally on our way."

"It's all so green."

"Green and wet and beautiful." He lifted his face to the watery sunlight. "I can smell rain."

"I can't remember the last time I saw rain. I think it might have been during the monsoon, a year or so back. But I don't want that kind of downpour. I want a cold, steady rain, the kind that leaves you in no doubt that it's going to settle in for a while."

The boat moved slowly northward, leaving a fantail of white foam in its wake. Behind us, the deck was busy with hands securing the piles of wood required for fuel. Valentin had charmed the captain into selling one of the handful of berths available. It had taken some creative arranging to accommodate two narrow cots and our few belongings in the tiny, dark cabin but we'd succeeded. Nonetheless, I hoped for kind weather because I didn't relish being confined there for long stretches — certainly not for three or four months. The commanding officer of the garrison at the fort had kindly given us several books before our departure, all in French. Anything was better than reading the Koran…again.

The Captain had explained that there would be two

meals a day — a breakfast of bread and tea and an evening meal, which would be whatever the boat's cook managed to procure in the port of the day. We were, he explained, welcome to disembark at any of the stops to buy our own provisions. The mess was another tiny space, little more than a long table with benches, with just about enough room to accommodate the officers and us.

I watched the flat, delta landscape crawl past. A scoop of pelicans took flight at the boat's approach, climbing slowly into the silvery late afternoon sky. Further up the deck, the cook had a line suspended in the water, hoping to take advantage of the abundant fish.

"We should eat well tonight." Valentin eyed the cook, who'd already landed a pair of sturgeons. "I hope there's no bloody rice."

"So do I."

"Fried potatoes would be nice. Nothing fancy, just potatoes."

"Stop, you're making me hungry."

"I'm hungry too, but not necessarily for food." The heat in his voice was mirrored by his eyes, his intent unmistakable.

I took a deep breath, and curled my fingers around the rail. "Is that all you can think about? Haven't we already had this discussion?"

Valentin sighed, a trifle theatrically. "I thought I'd just make sure. It's going to be very hard to share that tiny cabin with you for so long and not..."

"You can always sleep on the deck." I tried to disregard my body's reaction to his words.

"Are you sure you want that?" He glanced at my trousers, at the bulge there. "I think your words say one thing and your body says another."

"Damn you."

"It's time we had a little sleep before dinner, don't you think? After all, everyone is busy. We'll only get in the way if we remain on deck."

I swallowed and looked for an answer in the murmuring

123

reeds along the river bank. I couldn't use my shoulder as an excuse because it was healing nicely and no longer caused me much grief. In any event, desire overruled what little common sense remained. "Just this once."

He grinned. "We'll see about that."

We slipped quietly below deck and along the narrow gangway toward our cabin, which was at the far end. Valentin shouldered the door open and pulled me in. I'd no sooner stepped in than he closed the door and pushed me against the wall, plunging his fingers into my hair.

I wrenched him close, wanting the pressure of his hips on mine. It was altogether too easy to grasp his arse, to feel them beneath my palms while he devoured my mouth with frantic kisses between fevered gasps for air.

"I have wanted this...you for so long." Valentin paused long enough to wrench my shirt off.

"Perhaps the bed would be a better place." I reached for his shirt and fumbled with the buttons, watching them yield to my touch. I planted kisses on his chest with each button freed, earning groans for my efforts. I dropped to my knees and released his cock from his trousers, stroking it, running my tongue around its gleaming head until he slid his hands beneath my arms and pulled me to my feet.

We reeled across the tight space and dropped onto the narrow bunk, discarding clothes until we paused and pressed flesh to flesh. Only then did the pace decrease, dictated by Valentin, who moved his hips with deliberate, tormenting slowness against mine. He punctuated his kisses with teasing little nips along my jaw, down my neck across my chest. All I could do was try to breathe, to keep him close.

He broke away and scrambled across the cabin. "Christ, I hope I can find the oil."

I propped myself up on my elbows and admired the long, pale sweep of his back, the way it curved smoothly toward his arse. Thin afternoon light slipped through the porthole and touched his hair, finding fire in it. A different fever burnt in me when he rose and turned, the bottle in his hand. He returned to the bed and pushed me back down before easing my legs apart and up, until my calves rested on his warm shoulders.

"I have wanted this…" He sighed.

"So have I." The confession slipped out when Valentin applied oil to his member, then to me, circling his fingers cautiously around my entrance.

My breath caught when he massaged his way into me, first one finger, then another. I gripped his upper arms. My hips rose to his touch. "Now…please."

Valentin nodded and withdrew his fingers before positioning his cock. The slick head burnt my sensitive flesh, made me want to beg for more. He plunged in.

I pulled his head down to mine, demanding more, wanting his attention. He obliged, covering my mouth with his own while he moved with agonizing care. I swept my hands over his shoulders, down his back, reveling in the warm silk of his skin. I grasped his arse and held him tight, keeping him inside me, reducing his thrusts to delicate, piercing jabs — each one touching that place inside that brought such pleasure. My balls tightened. I was already close to release.

Valentin stopped then rested his forehead on mine. Every breath touched my skin like a whisper. My body absorbed him, wanted to keep him there. Words I didn't dare speak, that I needed to deny circled my mind, threatened to spill from my lips. I silenced myself by kissing him, by sweeping my tongue over his. I wound my hand around his neck and inhaled the scent of him, the scent of sea air, of something indefinable and desirable.

He moved again, this time with more urgency, driving into me, withdrawing, gliding back in. Then he paused, dropped his head and pushed one last time. He groaned into my hair, finding release. I followed, spilling my seed between us. Valentin slumped onto me and was still. I stroked his hair and held him in silence while rain whispered against the murky glass of the porthole.

After a while he withdrew, then settled beside me. "Thank you."

"My pleasure." I slipped one leg between his.

He sat up and wrestled with the bedclothes until they were in place over us, enveloping us in warmth against the drizzly chill outside. The boat moved over the water, taking us north. I drew Valentin closer and decided that it was best just to go where the river took me.

* * * *

The dinner of sturgeon, fried potatoes and pickled cabbage left me exhausted. The after dinner glass of brandy, courtesy of the captain, deepened that tiredness. I excused myself from the crowded mess table, leaving Valentin deep in conversation with our host, and returned to our cabin, too tired to do anything other than undress and crawl gratefully into bed. I was in a half-doze by the time Valentin returned. The soft rustle of cloth followed by the gentle creak of the floorboards told me that he was undressing but I was far too weary to open my eyes and enjoy the sight. We had three or four months ahead of us, there would be plenty of time to appreciate what Valentin had to offer.

"Goodnight, Gabriel. Sleep well."

I felt the gentlest of warm touches on my forehead.

I mumbled a reply and pulled the covers to my neck before he extinguished the lamp. The gentle rocking of the boat soon lulled me to sleep.

* * * *

"Get them off me! Oh! Christ!"

I struggled out of the tangle of bedclothes and leaped to my feet, then groped for the lamp in the darkness. "Valentin?"

The flame spluttered and flared, illuminating the cabin. Valentin was sitting bolt upright on his bed, arms held over his face, as if he were warding something off.

"No, dear God, please. No more!" The shout became a defeated whine, full of fear. "Please leave me alone." He dragged his hands down his cheeks. The lamplight caught tears in his eyes. "For the love of God," he sobbed. "Save me."

"It's all right," I whispered. "It's just a bad dream." I sat on his bed and pulled his hands from his face. "Please... Valentin."

He tipped his head to one side, trailed his fingers over his skin, then looked at me...*really* looked at me. "Gabriel?"

"Yes. It's me." I held out my arms. "You're safe. You're on a boat now, heading home."

Valentin edged forward and fell into my embrace. He shook and clung to me while I stroked his sweat-dampened hair and whispered soothing words into his ear. "You must've remembered something. You must've dreamt of... that place."

"Cockroaches...beetles...spiders...and, oh Christ, the rats."

"In the Pit?"

He drew a deep shuddering breath. "Yes, and if that wasn't enough, the guards would throw more in every bloody day." Valentin pulled away and raked one hand across his chest. "Sometimes, I can still feel them...crawling over me."

I pulled him close once more. "It's over. You will never have to go back there again."

"I know." He pressed his cheek to my chest. "But why won't the dreams stop? I want them to stop."

I cradled him, holding him close. "I know you do. Perhaps they will. You know, the further away we get from there, the better."

He sighed and nestled against me. "I hope so."

"Don't worry. I'll be here if you need me."

"Will you sleep with me?" His voice sounded small, childlike.

"If that's what you want."

"It is." He lay down and eased me down beside him.

I gathered him up and held him, soothing the hair from his brow until he fell asleep.

* * * *

I woke to the weight of Valentin, still asleep, one arm thrown across my waist. Thin, gray light crept through the porthole. The deck above creaked and grumbled with the relentless footfalls of the crew. The captain shouted something in Russian. I idly wondered what time it was. I don't suppose it mattered much. I didn't want to move.

Valentin murmured and stirred, moving closer. His eyelids flickered open. "Hello. What are you doing here?"

"Keeping you company. You asked me to."

He sat up and ran one hand in his sleep-tousled hair. "I did?"

"You had a bad dream."

"I did?"

"You don't remember?"

He regarded me with wide eyes. "Not a thing."

I swung my legs around until my feet found the rough floorboards. "Perhaps it's just as well."

"It must've been very bad."

"It was." I rose, crossed the cabin then retrieved my clothes.

Valentin slumped on the edge of his bed. "Why can't I remember?"

"The mind is a strange place. Don't worry. It has passed and you're one day closer to home."

"I don't want too much time to think...to remember."

I finished dressing and sorted through our belongings. "Perhaps you should try and occupy your mind with one of these." I tossed the books that the garrison commander had given us onto his bed. "It might help."

He reached for his shirt then shrugged into it. I bid a

128

silent, longing farewell to his chest, wanting to cover it with kisses again.

"I suppose that might help. Or perhaps the cook would let me do the fishing. I'd like that." There was an echo of innocent hope in his voice.

"Perhaps he would. I'm partial to fishing myself."

"You are?"

"There's a nice little river on our estate. My brother and I used to spend a lot of time fishing for salmon." My mouth watered at the memory of Mrs Berry's poached salmon. Those days seemed a lifetime ago. "Our cook did wonderful things with anything that we caught."

"I've never had salmon."

"It's beautiful. The King of Fish."

"Ha! No, my friend, that would be sturgeon."

I pulled on my boots. "I suppose it's all right. I prefer the caviar."

Valentin fastened his trousers. "Oh yes. With blini. Now you are making me hungry."

My stomach rumbled.

"When we get to St Petersburg, I'll treat you to the finest caviar." He placed his hands on my shoulders and touched my lips with a brief kiss. "Washed down with French champagne."

"If you spoil me like that, I may not want to leave."

"Perhaps that's my intention." With that, he slipped into his boots and walked out of the door. "Now let's see about breakfast."

Chapter Eleven

The September rain fell as a gray drizzle on the streets of Tsaritsyn, turning the summer's dust to claggy mud.

"It'll be worth it." Valentin pushed up the hill. "We can buy supplies for the next leg of the trip."

I pulled the collar of my coat up to my cheeks in a pathetic attempt to ward off the autumnal chill. "It had better be. I'd rather be back on the boat."

"So would I, and we will be as soon as we pick up some decent cheese and sausages to go with the bread." He waved his bag at me, made lumpy by the addition of two loaves of black bread purchased from a baker.

I glanced past him, shivered and almost wished I was back in the muggy heat of Calcutta. "All these Cossacks make me nervous."

A raucous clump of them loitered on the corner.

"Don't worry, they're quite tame."

"Just because they're soldiers doesn't make them tame."

"You're perfectly safe." He grinned and moved closer until his shoulder brushed mine.

"I guess I'm just not used to being around so many people at once after so long."

"I know. I feel the same." He glanced over his shoulder. "They can be a bit lively when they've had a few drinks."

"That's what worries me."

As if to illustrate the point, a tall, ruddy-cheeked man reeled through the mud, wavering dangerously when he sidestepped a puddle. One of his colleagues swooped to his rescue, grabbing his friend's arm before hauling him out of harm's way.

"How badly do you want cheese?" Valentin asked.

"I can live without it."

He wheeled around. "Good, let's head back to the boat. I'm not in the mood for company, no matter how entertaining."

The cool breeze brought the scent of the river along the street. We splashed through the morass, avoiding passing horses or other passers-by.

"Yakolev?" The voice came from somewhere off to the side. "Am I seeing things?"

Valentin paused and glanced over his shoulder. "Bloody hell. What in God's name are you doing here?"

A man in an officer's uniform, gaudy with gold braid, strode toward us, deftly avoiding the puddles. He held his hand out in greeting. "What a remarkable surprise."

"Indeed." Valentin's reply was less effusive. The color faded from his cheeks. "I had no idea you were here. I thought you were in St Petersburg."

"I was, but they decided to send me here for my sins." The officer patted Valentin's shoulder. "What about you? Last I heard you were in Kabul causing trouble between the locals and the British."

Something kicked me in the gut. I stared at the officer, then at Valentin. "Really?"

"Scurrilous gossip." He shouldered the bag and shoved his hands into his coat pockets.

"You were in Kabul?" It was all I could do to spit the words out. So Akmal hadn't been wrong.

"Not here...please." There was something akin to fear in Valentin's eyes.

Good.

"I'll leave you two gentlemen to your reunion. I think I'll make my way back to the boat now." I nodded to them both, then turned and headed down the hill back toward the river. My thoughts were a mess, memories of friends — all dead, either in battle or killed during the retreat — the Abbotts who'd always taken pity on me and invited me to dinner on Sundays. Men I'd drank with, laughed with.

Dead. And the man I traveled with, whose life I'd saved, had their blood on his hands.

I hurried through the mud, not caring about puddles or the miserable drenching rain. I'd get back to the boat, gather my things together and disembark. There would be another boat along soon enough. I'd make my own way to Moscow, or St Petersburg and travel home from there.

Lesson learnt.

"Gabriel." Valentin's voice cut through the mess of memories and half-formed plans. "Wait."

I put my head down and kept walking. I wanted to be sick.

"I said wait." He grabbed my arm.

"No." I shook it off and quickened my pace, the boat in sight. The deck alive with activity, the clatter of firewood and the occasional curse or shouted order. "Just let me get my things and I'll let you travel home on your own."

"Don't be stupid."

I stopped and spun around. "Stupid? Stupid? I think it's clear that it's too late for me to do anything more stupid than I've already done. Christ! How could you keep such a secret all this time? Why the hell did I bother risking my neck to save yours? Had I known what you'd done, I would've left you there to rot." I curled my fingers into my palms until the nails found flesh and bit down. "My God, I've slept with a man responsible for the deaths of so many good people, so many innocent people. How dare you tell me not to be stupid? Leaving the boat will be the smartest thing I've done since I met you."

The wind plucked at Valentin's hair, sweeping it across his pale forehead. Haunted eyes stared back at me, wide and as dark and unreadable as the river water. "You don't know the whole story. Gustaffson was talking rubbish."

"I don't want to know the whole story. I think I've heard enough, don't you?" I turned my back on him once more and splashed my way down the hill, ignoring the rain that chilled my skin. The prospect of a warm, dry berth now a distant wish. If I was lucky, I could find a room in a hotel for a day or two.

"Christ, Gabriel. Please." He grabbed my arm once more, coiling his through the crook of my elbow. "Please hear me out."

Steam drifted idly from the dark narrow funnel of the boat. The captain leaned on the rail watching goods being hauled aboard. He just about looked ready for the off. I hoped I'd have time to collect my belongings. I put my head down. "There's nothing you can say. Just let me get on that boat and get my things. I don't need to hear any more of your fairy stories."

The gangplank was in sight and, for the moment, clear. I pulled away from Valentin's grip and hurried along it, my feet heavy on the rain-slicked wood.

"Gentlemen." The captain doffed his cap when we swept past with scarce nods to acknowledge his greeting.

Valentin followed me down the steep steps below deck, haunting my footfalls along the passage to our berth. I flung the door open and made for the pathetic bundle of belongings that marked the sum total of my past few months of traveling. Thank Christ it would be over before too long. If I was lucky, I could be back in Ireland before Christmas. If not, I had friends in France, in Italy. I had boltholes I could retreat to.

The door shut with an emphatic *thunk*. When I glanced around, Valentin was pressed against it, fingers splayed over the rough wood. His chest rose and fell rapidly. "Gabriel—"

"Shut up. For Christ's sake, just don't say anything. I just want to be away. I don't want any more reminders of the mistakes I've made."

"I won't let you leave."

I pulled my knife from my bundle and whipped it from its worn, leather sheath. "You bloody will." I was across the cabin in an instant, and a second later held the blade to his throat. "If you don't let me leave, I'll cut your throat and I won't regret it at all."

"Oh, spare me the drama. You'd murder a Russian officer in a garrison town overrun by Cossacks? Do you think you'd get out of here in one piece?"

"I'm not sure I care."

He reached up, curled his hand around my wrist and pushed my hand away. The fight drained out of me. Outside, the rattle of a large chain and the shouts of deckhands heralded the boat's departure. "I'll get off at the next stop, then. Just let me get my things together and I'll find somewhere else to sleep."

"No chance of that. We had the last berth, remember?"

"I'll sleep on the bloody deck if I have to."

"Don't be stupid. Autumn's coming. You've forgotten how cold it is outside India, my friend. Stay here with me and give me the benefit of the doubt. Just listen to me."

"I lost many friends in Kabul, there were women and children. Innocent people killed because the locals decided they'd had enough of us, because someone had been pouring poison into their ears." I forced myself to look him in the eyes. "Were you that someone?"

Valentin swallowed. My pulse pounded in my ears in the heavy silence of the cabin. I watched thoughts race over his face, watched him while he opened his mouth. "I...I was one of them...yes."

I let the knife drop to the floor. I could no longer look at him. Betrayal tore at my guts. If Calcutta ever found out that I'd helped to free a man who'd been responsible, albeit indirectly, for so many deaths, they'd... If they thought I was still alive, I wouldn't be for long. I'd be hung for treason. "How can you even have the gall to look me in the eye? Do you know how many people you killed?"

He dropped his gaze to the floor.

"That friend of mine in Bukhara, the one who brought us supplies, helped us, helped me care for you when you were released. He lost everything because someone had told the locals he was collaborating with us. That's why I wasn't in

Kabul when it fell, because I'd already been to Bukhara to help him settle into his new life. He and his family were lucky to escape with their lives after a mob burnt his house down."

I picked up the knife and walked away from him, to the porthole, watching the muddy little town slide away. The boat swayed gently before moving forward, gliding through the swirling brown expanse of water. I wished I'd never laid eyes on Tsaritsyn, let alone set foot in it. Our little idyll, the one I'd fooled myself with, was over.

"I was doing what I was told." Valentin pronounced each word slowly, carefully, quietly. "We all have our orders, Gabriel."

I trailed my fingers around the edge of the glass, feeling the chill beneath my fingertips. "I don't want to discuss this any further. I don't want to hear your voice. I don't want to see you because every time I'll look at you from now on, I'll just see my own stupidity and foolishness."

"I may be a bit difficult to avoid."

"I'll leave the boat at the next port. Then it will be easy."

"You'll travel across Russia on your own with winter coming. You *are* a fool."

"I'd rather be a frozen fool."

"Fine, I'll leave you to it." The door opened with a protesting creak then slammed a moment later. When I turned around, Valentin had gone.

* * * *

I stared at the wooden planks on the ceiling, following the knots and swirls of pine. Overhead, the deck was quiet, the only sound the relentless chugging of the engine propelling the boat through the currents. The damp gray afternoon had faded to twilight. I debated whether it was worth lighting a lamp but decided against it. The thought of seeking refuge in darkness held a certain attraction. If Valentin returned, I wouldn't have to look at him, wouldn't have to remind myself how much I wanted him.

I tried to work out where the next destination would be, how I would make myself to the nearest port and find my way back to Ireland. I wanted nothing more than to be in that cottage, listening to the constant whisper of the waves, the wind whistling down the chimney, the firelight dancing in the draft. But even there, I knew I'd remember, would never forget, would forever nurse the pain of betrayal.

Rain splattered against the glass. I rolled over and closed my eyes. If nothing else, there was always sleep. In sleep it was possible to forget everything. I drifted off, reaching for dreams of home, for green grass and soft weather, of refuge from the hurt.

* * * *

"Oh look, he's still here." Valentin's words all ran together. The reek of brandy stole across the cabin.

There followed a great deal of clattering, thumping, cursing and sighs. Then, uncertain light flickered into life. I sat up, still half-asleep and watched Valentin lurch across the floor, leaving a trail of discarded clothes in his wake. He sank onto his bed and stared at me, his eyes glittering with drunken good cheer. "I thought you were leaving."

"Oh do shut up. I'll leave in the morning while you're still sleeping your brandy off."

"Brandy." He leered and leaned forward with a wobble. "Good old brandy. So much better than bloody vodka."

I didn't answer.

Valentin shrugged. "Yessitis. The captain has some very fine brandy. You should've joined us. You might've enjoyed it."

"I doubt that."

"Miserable bastard." He flopped back onto the bed, arms spread wide across the rumpled covers. "By God, you're a miserable bastard. Very pleasing on the eyes but you don't bloody say much. You just sit there and you give me that stare…the one my bloody mother used to give me when I'd come home from yet another bloody ball without a fiancée in tow."

I rose and extinguished the lamp.

"Whaddya do tha' for?" His voice was all wounded puzzlement.

"You're drunk, I'm tired. I don't feel like looking at you and I certainly don't feel like listening to your meanderings. I'm hoping you'll take the hint and sleep."

The cot creaked, bedclothes whispered. Valentin's shadow shuffled around in the darkness. "Fine. Suit yourself."

I retreated to my bed. By the time my head hit the pillow, the cabin resonated with the breathy rattle of Valentin's heavy snores.

Once I was certain that he slept, I got up once more and groped for the wash basin. As quietly as I could, I set it on the floor beside his bed, knowing the effect that brandy could have on one's constitution. Then, I dressed silently, slipped into my boots, grabbed my coat and sought refuge on the quiet deck.

The night wind smelled of autumn, of mist and damp soil, even though the banks were hundreds of feet away on either side. The boat chugged northwards beneath a sky ragged with broken clouds. The thin crescent of moon appeared now and then. I watched for it while I leaned on the railing. At least it was a dry night. After a while, I left the railing and searched for a dry place on the deck. There was a place, a little bit of canvas where a few pieces of firewood had been stored. I rearranged them, making enough space to sit. After a few moments of fidgeting, I wrapped my arms around my legs, rested my chin on my knees and closed my eyes. It wasn't much, but it was better than sharing the tiny cabin with the reek of stale brandy and the snores of a drunken Russian bastard.

* * * *

Something nudged my foot. I woke with a start and looked up from my shelter to see the captain smirking at me.

"So there you are. His lordship has been threatening to tear my boat apart looking for you."

I rubbed my sore neck. "Well now there's no need. You can tell him that you found me."

"You can tell him yourself, mate. I have a boat to look after." He stepped back and held out his hand to help me scrabble to my feet.

"I don't suppose there's another cabin available is there?"

"What's the matter? Is he getting on your nerves?"

"Something like that, yes."

He scratched at his beard and stared past me. "There's a tiny space. I could just about fit you in there. It wouldn't be very comfortable, mind."

"It can't be worse than where I've just slept." I would've happily slept on a pile of wood.

"No, it's better than that...just. It's at the stern end. Just storage really, but only when I've too much on board. I can get one of the lads to cram that cot in there."

"That'll be fine. I'll pay you, of course. I only intend to use it until we reach the next port. I'll get off there, then wait for the next boat, if it's not too long."

"The *Russalka* is about three days behind us. You should be able to get a berth on there."

"Thanks, then that's what I'll do."

He grinned. "Fine, I'll get someone to sort it out for you. In the meantime, I suggest you go and reassure your friend that you didn't fall overboard in the middle of the night."

"Yeah, right. I will." I walked away from him, reluctant to leave the damp, cold air and return to the drama that waited for me below deck.

* * * *

"Where the hell have you been?" Valentin stood in the

138

middle of the cabin, hair mussed, eyes red-rimmed. The odor of stale brandy hung like a miasma in the small space.

"Sleeping." I swept past him and scraped all my belongings together, shoving them hastily into my bag.

"Where?"

"Does it matter?" I clenched my hands around my bag in an attempt to avoid hitting him.

"It does to me."

"Leave it, Valentin. I've found somewhere else to sleep. If I were you, I'd leave me alone for the remainder of this voyage. I've heard all I want to hear from you. Our debt to each other is discharged." I glanced away from the hurt and bewilderment in his eyes. "I'll make my own way home."

"But…how?"

"I'll manage." I made for the door, anxious to escape the pain of his presence.

"Gabriel…please."

"No." I slammed the door on him and walked away, hoping he'd leave me alone.

Chapter Twelve

The captain of the *Russalka* tugged absently at his beard and surveyed the river. "I think this is as far as we can go."

I shivered in the snowy wind. "How far is it from here to Moscow?"

He shrugged. "Probably about ten days by troika. You should be able to hire one here."

The lights of Nizhny Novgorod glittered gold in the lowering November twilight. There were worse places for a river journey to end. After two and a half months in a cramped cabin, eating basic fare and passing the time by helping the crew, I was ready for a night or two in decent lodgings, a hot bath and a soft, warm bed before traveling on again.

I held my hand out to the captain. "Thank you for everything. It's been a pleasant trip."

He shook it, his grin huge. "My pleasure, sir. It's been good to enjoy such interesting company for a change."

I gathered my things together and headed for the gangplank, which was already dusted with white. An icy wind blew from the river, sending flurries of snow across the dock. I pulled the collar of my coat up and kept walking, toward the heart of the town and the lodgings the captain had recommended. He had assured me that it was one of the better places and that they would be able to arrange a troika for me, when I was ready to travel. All I could think of a warm, comfortable bed and a decent meal. Things I would never take for granted again.

In spite of the weather, the streets were alive with people and chatter. After so long on the boat, it seemed strange to be amongst crowds again. The aroma of baking bread drifted with the breeze, then something savory, reminding me that I hadn't eaten since breakfast. I hurried along, driven by hunger. I glanced at the scrap of paper the captain had given me, with hastily scribbled directions. The Cyrillic script was hard to make out in the waning light, so I paused for a moment, looking for the landmark I was to turn left beside. The building appeared out of the snow ahead of me. I pocketed the paper and strode on, kicking through the powder.

The hotel sign swung in the wind and light spilt onto the street like a promise. I ignored the brush off a passer-by and smiled with relief. A real bed and a good meal waited for me. It almost felt as if my journey was coming close to the end.

* * * *

I admired the meal set before me — a bowl of stew, redolent with cabbage, a loaf of black bread, butter, cheese and a bottle of wine. It was more than I could've possibly wished for. I resolved to send a note to the captain of the *Russalka* by way of thanks. After a hot bath in a beaten tin tub and a change of clothes, the feast seemed the most fitting way to celebrate the end of another stage of the journey home. I tore off a piece of bread and dipped it into the rich broth of the stew. I intended to savor every mouthful.

The small dining room was quiet, the silence broken only by the occasional rattle of the window when gusts of wind slammed snow into the panes. I didn't look up when the door opened, admitting a draft and swirl of flakes. The chill lingered long after the door snicked shut.

"Gabriel." The bread fell into the bowl. Valentin, hair damp with snow, leaned on the table and retrieved it before popping it into his mouth.

"What the hell are you doing here?"

"Waiting for you."

I set my spoon down and reached for my wine. Needing it. "Why?"

"Because I've had a lot of time to think, that's why."

My heart raced. I wrapped my fingers around the stem of the glass and took a long, deep draft. "I've spent the last few months putting everything, including you behind me. I would rather not have the whole sorry business raked over again. Can't you just let me go home in peace?"

Valentin glanced over his shoulder then covered my hand with his. "No, not until we've spoken without anger."

"I can't believe you waited, hoping I would turn up."

"This is the only decent lodging house in the place. I hoped that you'd have the sense to seek it out. The captain told me that you were on the *Russalka*. I knew all I'd have to do was wait a few days."

"I would've thought you'd be anxious to get home."

"Not without talking to you first. I want to clear the air."

In spite of the fluttering in my gut, hunger won out. I reached for my spoon and took a mouthful of stew. I ignored Valentin's desperate stare and enjoyed the taste of rich broth, tender meat and cabbage. "All right. But can I eat first? This is the first decent meal I've eaten since we left Bukhara."

"Fine. I can wait." He folded his arms and leaned back in his chair.

"Are you going to watch me eat? I'm not sure I want an audience."

"I just want to make sure you don't slip away again."

"Am I that important to you?" Another mouthful of stew, some barley and a shred of onion.

"Yes."

There was no answer to that. Instead, I helped myself to another piece of bread. The scent of fermented yeast and licorice bite of caraway rose to meet me. I was determined to enjoy every bloody bite of that meal, so I did, while my companion plucked impatiently at a heel of bread and watched the snow slide down the night-blackened window.

Finally, I pushed the empty bowl away and drained the last of my wine. "All right, then. Start talking. It's been a long day and I'm very tired."

He glanced over his shoulder again. "Can we talk somewhere more private?"

"Where did you have in mind?" I knew damn well what he was about to suggest.

"Your room."

"As long as you don't intend to seduce me."

"No. I promise. I won't." He stood and waited.

I stood slowly, guts churning. I'd spent so much time on the *Russalka* pushing the memories of him away, pushing aside feelings that had no place with me, feelings that would lead nowhere.

He followed me up the narrow, shadowed staircase and along the corridor to my room. While I'd been dining, someone had come in and added more wood to the small stove in the corner. It radiated a comforting warmth that, combined with the meal, conspired to make me sleepy. I propped the feather bolster against the headboard and sank onto the bed while Valentin settled into the chair beside the stove, hands clasped over his stomach. I waited, noting how thin and pale he'd become. The pain in his eyes surprised me. I wondered if it echoed mine.

"Go on. Make this short please. I'm very tired."

"It's all right, this won't take long." He sighed and stared at his knees.

"Good." I leaned back into the bolster and waited.

His shoulders rose and fell. "I didn't want to go to Kabul. My job has never been about causing trouble. It has always been about going somewhere and observing. I don't like to interact with the 'locals', I don't feel comfortable, I don't trust my abilities, I just like to watch. So I didn't want that mission." He ran one hand through his hair. "There were two other...agents. I let them do all the talking. My job was simply to linger in public places and listen, to hear what the people were saying and planning, checking that my colleagues' words were bearing fruit. That was bad enough. I don't care much for the wholesale slaughter of anyone. That's not why I became an army officer. That was just me fulfilling my obligations to my family." He threw a defiant glance in my direction. "Isn't that why you joined the army?"

"Yes." The weight of my anger slowly slid away.

"As soon as I realized that my colleagues had succeeded in planting those seeds of dissent, there was no need to remain, so I left. I left long before the trouble started. I wanted no part of that." Valentin shook his head. "So to hear you say that I had the blood of your friends on my hands hurt, because it isn't true. But because I was there, because I worked with those who sought to cause trouble, I am sorry. But remember, you've also had do to things that you didn't approve of, haven't you?"

"All the bloody time," I conceded. My indignation no longer had anything to fuel it. I allowed myself to feel something other than disgust for him for the first time in months. "I'm sorry. I lost so many friends. It made me lose my taste for this work, made me wonder what the point was. These people don't want us there, why would we impose ourselves and our laws on them? It'll only lead to trouble in the end. The more we interfere, the more discord we'll cause."

"So you forgive me?"

"There's nothing to forgive." Relief swept through me. Finally, it was over. There was nothing between us but friendship and memories left, memories worth keeping.

"Thank you." His smile made the empty months worthwhile. For a moment I glimpsed that officer who'd ridden with such arrogance into the dusty courtyard of a small desert inn. Something inside skipped and fluttered.

Valentin pushed himself out of the chair. "Now, I shall let you sleep. I can see how tired you are."

"Is it that obvious?"

"Yes." He stooped to leave a kiss on my brow. "Goodnight,

144

vozulbleny. Sleep well."

"I will." I scarcely heard the whisper of his footsteps when he left the room. By the time he closed the door gently behind him, I'd closed my eyes scarcely taking in the fact that he'd called me 'beloved'.

* * * *

Pale light flooded the room. I rose, dressed and splashed cold water on my face before peering through the frosted window glass. The street below was deep with snow. The surrounding rooftops were swathed in it and more fell, drifting idly down in fat flakes. I leaned against the wall beside the stove and enjoyed its warmth while I could. There was the small matter of a troika to arrange.

A gentle knock on the door heralded the arrival of breakfast—black bread warm from the oven, a generous pat of butter and some kind of berry preserve. The lad set it on the cabinet and exited with a nod and a smile. I left the stove and poured myself a glass of tea before sitting down to enjoy a leisurely repast, in no hurry to do anything or go anywhere. The novelty of remaining in one place was almost too much to resist. It was nice to stare out of a window and realize that I wasn't on something that was in motion.

By the time I'd finished breakfast, the snow had eased to a light flurry. I washed and shaved with the hot water that had been delivered, then retrieved my coat. I wondered whether I should seek Valentin out, but decided against it. I knew that the more time I spent in his company, the less likely I'd want to leave it. I had to think about getting home.

I'd no sooner stepped out of my room than Valentin had made the decision for me.

"Good morning." He rubbed his cheek and offered me an uncertain smile. "Are you going for a stroll?"

"I am going to find a troika for hire so that I can travel to Moscow."

"You don't need to do that. It's already arranged."

"There you go again, taking liberties. Making decisions for me." A little bit of relief that the work was taken from my hands slid over me.

"It seems to make sense that we travel together. Share a troika. It will be nice to have the company."

"As long as company is all you want." More relief, knowing that I wouldn't be traveling alone. It worried me that the prospect had become something I hadn't looked forward to.

He held his hands, palms up. "That is all I want. Nothing else. Friends, yes?"

"Yes...friends." The rest, I would have to learn to leave behind.

Chapter Thirteen

Our driver, a very well-fed bearded bear of a man gave us a gap-toothed grin. "Are you ready, gentlemen?"

I settled into the seat. Valentin arranged the furs we'd bought around our legs. "Yes, we're ready."

The horses, three bays, pawed at the hard-packed snow, in a fever to be away. Harness bells jingled in a silvery little song while our breath rose into the cold, bright morning air.

"Excellent." The driver, Yuri, called to the horses. They sprang forward as one and the troika lurched then glided along the track.

"This is the way to travel." Valentin adjusted the furs once more. "Not too cold and a damn sight quicker than a bloody boat."

I was about to dispute the point about the cold but thought better of it, choosing instead to wind my scarf closer around my head. The furs certainly worked. Valentin's leg rested against mine but it didn't matter because his gloved hands were in clear view. I was not about to let him talk or touch his way into my bed again.

"Yes, it is." The unaccustomed speed was exhilarating. The wind bit into my cheeks but it didn't matter.

"It won't take long."

"Good." I watched the fringe of the town slip away, opening onto a flat, featureless plain. The horses raced each other, manes flying as they galloped along the track. The world whipped by in a snowy, brilliant blur.

Valentin placed his hand over mine. "Happy?"

"Yes." I was. Every mile we traveled put the nightmares

farther behind me.

"Good." He pressed his leg against mine beneath the furs. "Then let's enjoy this journey. It is nearly over."

I almost wished that we were alone. The heat of his leg brought with it a rush of long-denied desire. I took a deep breath and held it, while trying to think of something else, a cold bath, rotten fruit…an overlong Sunday morning mass. Then Yuri leaned over the side of the troika and spat theatrically. That quenched the fire more quickly than it had arisen.

Valentin moved closer. "I've been thinking," he whispered, his breath warm on my cheek.

"That's not good…you thinking. What have you been thinking about?"

"You."

"Valentin—"

"Wait. I'll tell you tonight. Don't worry. I don't plan on seducing you…yet." He drew away, but not before brushing my cold earlobe with his warm lips in parting. I turned my attention to the snow-covered landscaped and tried to will my erection away.

* * * *

"It's a bit rough, but at least it's warm." Valentin collapsed onto the bed.

"There's only one bed."

"For sleeping." He sat up, resting against the wall. "That's all. I told you I had no plans to seduce you."

"What did you plan?" I sat down beside him, tempting fate, inviting temptation.

He drew a deep breath and inched closer until his shoulder touched mine. "I want to start all over again, as if we'd just met, as if we had no history between us."

It was hard to deny the hopeful note in his voice.

"To what end? I'm going home. You're going home."

"I was hoping to persuade you to stay with me, at least

148

until spring. Then if you like, you can go. Your journey home will be less trying in warmer weather."

"You'd like me to stay, in your *dacha*, in the forest."

"Very much." Valentin picked up my hand and held it. I closed my eyes when he lightly brushed his thumb over my skin.

"Life is too short, Gabriel. We should enjoy what we can while we can. When you return home, we'll never see each other again. I don't want to think beyond that moment, I want to enjoy the time left to us. Is that too much to ask?"

I considered this while he held onto my hand and stroked it. A piece of green wood popped and crackled in the belly of the stove. "So tell me about this place of yours, tell me why I should spend the winter there."

He kept hold of my hand. "It's not big, as I think I've mentioned. But there are stoves in every room and plenty of firewood. There's a couple — Sergei and Anya — they look after the place for me. They're very discreet and Anya is a very fine cook. They'll leave us in peace." Valentin rested his head on my shoulder. "Wouldn't that be nice?"

"Very nice. Do they know of your…?"

"My preferences? Yes. That's why I employ them, because they would never tell a soul. It helps that I pay them well, I suppose." He nestled closer. "It's so peaceful there, in the middle of a birch forest. The snow gets so deep and everything is muffled in silence. I can't wait to get there."

I turned and kissed the top of his head. "I don't blame you. But don't you think we'd drive each other mad if we were confined together for such a long time?"

"No. I couldn't think of anything more pleasurable."

"You make it sound very appealing."

"That's because it is."

I tried to imagine the possibilities — the pleasure of being courted rather than seduced "I'm in no hurry to get home and have to explain myself to my brother. I've forgiven you for your transgressions. I suppose it's worth pursuing."

"You make it sound so clinical."

"I'm trying to be sensible, which isn't always easy in your presence."

He laughed softly. "Should I be flattered?"

"Yes." I rested my cheek on his head and listened to the window rattling in the frame. "I'm used to being on my own, to living on my own."

"Yet you're giving my proposal serious thought?"

"I am."

"Thank you." He sat up, swung his legs to the floor and stood up. "I'm tired, I need to sleep. Do you feel safe enough to share the bed with me?"

"Of course I do."

"Good." He kicked off his boots, then unfastened his trousers.

I followed his example, hurrying out of my clothes before diving beneath the covers.

"We could have a whole winter of this." Valentin threw his arm over my waist. "Keeping warm, just...talking."

"Keep going, you are very persuasive."

"What else shall I tell you?"

"Tell me how you plan to win me over, how you plan to court me."

"You'll have to wait and see. I want to do it properly." He lifted his head. "I want to do right by you, Gabriel. I nearly lost you. I don't want that to happen again."

My resolve crumbled just a bit. I pushed the hair from his forehead. "No more secrets, then. No more melodrama."

"All right. I'll try. I can't promise anything."

I settled closer to him, tired from the long, cold journey. "I look forward to being wooed, but I think we should sleep."

"You are too sensible." Valentin kissed my shoulder then closed his eyes. "We'll have to work on that."

"How do you propose to change my sensibilities?"

"Well, before we go to the *dacha*, we will need to stop in St Petersburg. My mother will need to know that I'm alive. We can rest there for a few days, while someone sends word to the *dacha*. Then, after a few days, we can go and your education can begin."

"You're taking me to meet your mother?"

"Don't worry. I will introduce you as a good friend, the man who saved me from the Emir's dungeons. You'll be welcomed as a hero and offered a home for life."

"That seems a bit...effusive."

"You'll understand when you meet her."

"I can't wait." My eyelids grew heavy. I'd worry about the implications of meeting Valentin's mother when I was less tired, less mesmerized by the man who rested beside me.

Chapter Fourteen

The troika driver eased the horses to a halt in front of the tall house beside the canal. Lights glittered on the dark water and the windows glowed golden in the dusk.

"Here we are." Valentin stepped down and gathered his belongings. "Are you ready to meet her?"

I swallowed and glanced at the door at the top of the steps. Snow fell from a wintry sky. "I suppose so."

Valentin paid the troika driver then headed for the steps. Before he could reach the top, the door swung open and a liveried servant stood in the doorway. "Master...this is a surprise."

"Excellent. That's what I wanted."

"Shall I tell your mother you're here?"

"If you wouldn't mind. Could you also arrange for a room for my friend here? We've had a very long and tiring journey."

I managed a thin smile and stared past the servant to the long, well lit hall beyond. A generous blast of warmth embraced me when I followed Valentin into the foyer. Everything gleamed, everything shone, from the glittering chandelier to the polished floor. The broad staircase was adorned with portraits, an ascending row of stern faces staring coldly at new arrivals. I thought of my ancestral pile with its faded rugs, lounging hunting dogs and the vague chaos that my brother had inherited. The servant left us, hurrying along the corridor to a door at the far end. He knocked then disappeared into the room.

Valentin set his bags down and touched my hand. "Brace yourself."

Moments later the door opened and a woman, elegant in a silk gown, hurried toward us, arms held out. "Oh darling, Valya. What a wonderful surprise!" She swept him up in an excited embrace. "I'm so glad you're here. I've been *so* worried. No one has heard from you."

"It's been a little...difficult." Valentin stepped back. "But here we are, both safe and sound."

His mother turned and looked at me for the first time, surveying me with cool gray eyes, her son's eyes. "Who is this handsome gentleman?"

My cheeks burnt.

"This is Captain Gabriel O'Riordan. He is the man who saved my life. If it wasn't for him, I wouldn't be standing here right now."

My face flamed even more.

His mother extended a languid hand. "Really? You're not just telling tales are you, Valya?"

"No, Mother. When we've settled in, rested and changed, we'll tell you everything."

"Oh, do hurry then. I want to hear everything. Come into the parlor and have a drink while your rooms are being prepared. You must both be perished. It's so *dreadfully* cold today." She took my arm, and Valentin's and steered us along the hall into a firelit room that was almost suffocating in its warmth.

I sank gratefully into a chair while Madame Yakoleva summoned a servant and requested refreshments. Valentin regarded me with a quirk of an eyebrow and sat back, apparently more than happy to let his mother make a fuss of him. In moments, a maid appeared carrying a tray rattling with cups and plates laden with delicate little pastries and sandwiches. I was instantly reminded of tea with the Abbotts, when Mrs Abbott had gone out of her way to produce a proper English tea in Kabul. I fought the memory and thanked Madame Yakoleva when she passed me a cup, and a plate piled high with food.

"You must both eat. Valya, you look like you've lost

weight. You need to look after yourself."

"Yes, mother. I will. I've been telling Gabriel about the wonderful food. We're both eagerly anticipating a splendid meal or two."

"I hope it will be more than just a few. You will be staying won't you?"

"Just for a little while. I would like to spend the winter at the *dacha*. I need peace and quiet. You'll understand why when we tell you our tale."

"Oh dear, must you? I don't know how you can bear to stay out there for so long. It's fine in the summer for a week or two, but it must be so dreary in the winter."

"It's very peaceful. That's what I...we need. Gabriel will be staying with me, at least until spring. We just need to rest. We've done nothing but travel for months."

"Well...if that's what you want. I'd rather you weren't such a hermit dear, but I understand. I'll send word to Sergei and Anya to get things ready for you both. In the meantime you must rest here, enjoy yourselves."

"We will. Thank you."

"We'll have a wonderful time."

I plucked a sandwich from the plate, a thin little thing filled with smoked fish. I wanted more, wanted to lose myself in luxury after months of privation. I almost wept with the simple joy of that little sandwich and sitting in a warm room while winter settled around the house.

Moments later another servant appeared at the door to announce that our rooms were ready. I was grateful to reach the room allotted to me. I leaned against the closed door and tried to take it all in — the enormous bed, covered with a heavy silk canopy, the large stove in the corner throwing out generous warmth, the large tin tub sitting in front of it, filled with steaming water.

I stripped and jumped into the bath, sinking into the blessed heat. What little chill remained in my bones after the journey was soon washed away. I rested my head on the back of the tub and closed my eyes.

A soft rap on the door interrupted my reverie. The servant reappeared bearing an armload of clothes.

"Master Valentin thought that you might like some clean clothes." He spread them out on the vast bed before scooping up my discarded garments and carrying them away, presumably to launder.

After a while, I left the bath and dried myself off in front of the stove, enjoying the warmth before dressing. I couldn't remember the last time I'd dressed for dinner. I couldn't remember the last time I'd sat down to a proper meal in a proper dining room, with servants and polite conversation.

While I was fiddling with the cravat, another knock disturbed my progress. Valentin stepped into the room then closed the door behind him. We stared at each other in silence for a moment or two.

"You look...handsome. Let me fix that." He stepped closer and adjusted my cravat. "I hate these things."

"So do I." I raised my chin to allow him access while he deftly rearranged the linen.

"There." Valentin stepped back and smiled. "All fixed."

"Thank you." I poked a finger beneath wretched constraint and loosened it slightly.

He extended a hand toward me, letting it glide over my cheek. "Yes, very handsome."

I leaned into his touch. "So are you."

"I am tired and travel weary. I'm sure it shows."

"No." I covered my hand with his. "It doesn't."

Valentin leaned forward and touched my lips with his, gently at first, then with more insistence.

I wound my fingers through his hair and pulled him closer.

He groaned softly and pressed his hips to mine, leaving me in no doubt how much he desired me. I certainly was in no doubt how much I desired him. I would've given anything to throw him down onto the bed, sink into the embrace of the soft linen and feel the fire of his skin against mine. Instead, we broke apart, hearing the stealthy tread of a servant in the hall outside.

"I suppose," he whispered, "we should go downstairs."

I swallowed. "Yes, I think we'd better."

"Don't worry. We'll have a whole winter." Valentin squeezed my hand then opened the door. "Let's go and have dinner."

* * * *

"Oh good heavens." Madam Yakoleva held her hand to her breast in a rather melodramatic fashion. "What a terrible ordeal. Oh, Valya…"

"You were very lucky." Valentin's brother, Piotr, took a long draft from his wine. "Very lucky."

"I know." Valentin's hand stole to my knee. "If it wasn't for Gabriel, I wouldn't be here."

Piotr raised his half-empty glass to me. "And we will always be grateful and always in your debt. Thank you. A lesser man would've walked away."

"I couldn't do that."

Madam Yakoleva reached across the table and clasped my hand. "And now you will be family to us. You will always be welcome here."

My cheeks burnt. "You are too kind." I wanted to be away from all the fuss. After months of being almost exclusively in the company of one man, the effusiveness of his family was too much. I should've been touched by their kindness and gratitude but it just made me feel…imprisoned.

"Mother, I think you must stop making a fuss. Poor Gabriel has turned quite red." Valentin squeezed my knee then withdrew his hand. He picked up his wine glass and took a sip.

I offered up a silent prayer of thanks. I turned my attention back to the meal, noticing how the chicken fell apart from the lightest touch. The aroma of herbs rose to meet me. After months of rice, then simple fare, Valentin's welcome home feast overwhelmed me with its richness and mosaic of flavors. I hoped that I wouldn't regret it the following day.

"So, Valya, what are your plans now?" Piotr waved for more wine.

Beside me, Valentin stilled. He set his knife and fork down and inhaled slowly. "When I have rested for a day or two, I shall prepare my report and take it to the Ministry. I'll also be resigning my commission."

Madam Yakolev gasped. "Oh, Valya. Are you sure?"

"Yes. I'm sure. I'm tired and I've had one brush with death too many. I intend to live simply at the *dacha*. I may even write a book about my adventures. You know I don't lead an extravagant life. I can manage very well on what Father left me, and on my pension."

"It's just as well." Piotr scowled into his wine. "You won't be expecting any help, will you?"

"No I will not. I'll be fine. You don't need to worry about me coming to you begging for funds."

"Don't worry, dear." Madam Yakolev squeezed Valentin's hand where it rested on the table. "I still have plenty of funds. If your brother won't help you, I will."

"It's all right, Mother. I doubt that it would ever come to that."

Piotr turned his attention to me. "What about you, sir? What are your intentions?"

"My employers believe I'm dead. I see no reason to disabuse them of that notion. I have no intention of returning to my former duties. As Valentin said, it's a dangerous occupation and we can only cheat death so many times. When spring comes, I'll probably return to Ireland and live an equally quiet and simple life."

He raised an eyebrow. "How extraordinary. You both have occupations that many would dream of — to travel to fascinating places, to work outside the confines of an office, to see things that we can only read about and yet you both have decided that enough is enough at a relatively young age."

"I should like to survive long enough to grow old," I replied. "Espionage is not an occupation for old men. I have given the job several years of my life and, yes, I've been fortunate to see many wondrous things, but I've also lost many, many comrades and friends."

"I think you are both wise." Madam Yakoleva chased a piece of meat around her plate with her fork. "I would rather you both enjoyed long and happy lives than risk them."

Piotr glared across the table at his brother. "Perhaps you could request a desk job."

Valentin's knuckles turned white when he clenched his fork. "I could. But I don't want to. After years of working out in the field, the prospect of sitting in an office day after day seems no better than a living death. I'm sorry, brother. I know that you're happy enough with your occupation, but it isn't for me. I am no bureaucrat."

"Well, if that's what you want." His brother shrugged and addressed his dinner once more. "You won't find yourself a wife that way."

"I don't want a wife. I don't want children. I am not interested."

Madam Yakolev sighed somewhat theatrically and signaled to a footman for more wine. "I don't know why you're so adamant about not getting married. You could have your pick of eligible young women."

Valentin stabbed at a potato. "I know. But I'm not going to. Anyway, I can't imagine any young lady wishing to spend most of her days in the countryside, which is what I intend to do."

"I had so wanted to see you married, Valya." Disappointment colored every word. "You know how much I'd love grandchildren."

"Which I am sure my brother will be happy to provide when he finally settles on a wife."

Valentin's curt words earned another harsh stare from his brother. I set down my knife and fork, my appetite soured.

"I am courting Elena Zykova." Piotr grunted, pushing his empty plate away. The flickering light from the chandelier caught the sudden flush of his pale, slightly plump cheeks. "In fact, I am escorting her to a party tomorrow night. I have every intention of proposing to her."

"At least you've finally made up your mind," Valentin observed. "I was beginning to wonder."

"I intend to propose at Christmas. I've already spoken with her father."

"That's wonderful news!" Madam Yakolev clasped her hands together, leaned over and kissed her eldest son on the cheek. "I think we need champagne tonight. My youngest son made it safely home and my eldest is about to propose. I couldn't be happier." She turned in her chair. "Mikhail, could you bring some champagne please?"

The butler nodded toward a footman who then hurried out of the room. I hoped that the champagne would do something to dispel the tension.

* * * *

I stared at the man who sat on the other side of the vast, polished desk. The wintry sunlight glittered on the gold braid of his uniform. "I'm sorry. Could you say that again?"

"I said that, because of your selfless bravery in saving Captain Yakolev at risk to your own life, you will be paid a reward and will be receiving an annual stipend for as long as you choose to remain in Russia."

"Good heavens. Really?"

The Adjutant General pushed a leather pouch across the desk. "Here is the first payment. I think you will find it most generous."

I didn't dare touch it. I couldn't. I'd never even thought of money but I supposed I would need it. "Thank you. I really hadn't expected...this."

"The Tsar is most grateful. He wanted to reward you in some way."

"Please convey my thanks and gratitude." I reached reluctantly for the pouch and tucked it in my coat.

My host rose, signaling an end to our little meeting. I followed suit and shook his proffered hand.

"I wish you well, Captain O'Riordan. I hope you will enjoy your stay in Russia. I'm sorry to hear that Captain Yakolev has resigned his commission but, in the circumstances, I can understand. He was a very fine agent, our best by a long way."

"Yes, sir." I wanted to ask him about Kabul. I wanted to know if Valentin had told me the truth or whether he'd just told me a fairy tale to placate me. I looked at the Adjutant General and knew that I'd be a fool for asking. I pushed it all to the back of my mind, suddenly too tired to pursue the matter. Perhaps some things were best left buried.

He offered me a smile. "Should either of you change your minds or get bored of your lives of leisure, there will always be work for you."

"Not for me, sir. I may have deceived my government by letting them believe that I'm dead, but I could serve no other country."

"I understand the sentiment and commend you for it. That, my friend, was the correct answer." He patted my shoulder with some warmth then steered me toward the door. "Goodbye, Captain."

"Sir." I saluted him, then slipped into the hall, to where Valentin waited.

He stood when I strode toward him. The wintry light fell through a window and caught in his hair. I almost forgot to breathe. He'd worn his uniform to the Ministry, and he looked every inch the hussar. I could almost sympathize with the Adjutant General's disappointment at losing such an officer.

"Everything all right?" He adjusted his pelisse.

"Absolutely."

"Really?" He raised an eyebrow.

"Yes, really."

"Because you had a funny look on your face for a minute or two." The devil was in his grin.

I glanced over my shoulder before walking on. "I did?"

"Like you'd glimpsed paradise."

"I'm not going to tell you. You have a high enough opinion of yourself as it is."

His laugh echoed along the corridor. "Oh, Gabriel. Really? Don't you want to feed my vanity just a bit more?"

"You know what I was thinking, what I *am* thinking, so I shan't bother elaborating."

He nudged me. "It's the uniform, isn't it?"

"You know it is." We hurried down a broad staircase. I was anxious to escape outdoors in the hope that the icy December air would cool my burning cheeks.

Valentin's boot heels echoed across the foyer. "Perhaps I shall keep it, then. Save it for special occasions." He winked and pushed the door open.

A bitter wind blew up the street. I shivered and pulled my coat tighter while Valentin waved for the troika. He stood close, close enough for me to feel some residual heat.

"Don't worry," he said as we climbed into the troika. "We'll soon be home."

"Good." I burrowed under the furs. "It can't come soon enough."

He covered my hand with his beneath the warm covers. "I tell you what can't soon enough, getting to the *dacha*."

"As long as it's warm."

He leaned close. "It will be. I'll see to that."

The touch of his breath on my cheek and the heat in his words were enough to stir my desire. "Is that a promise?"

"Yes. It's been very difficult, these past few days, living under my mother's roof, thinking very unwholesome thoughts about you." He moved his hand along my thigh, applying pressure with his palm.

"It's very difficult right at this moment." I took a deep breath and held onto it. "You're not helping."

"I like to see you like this. It reassures me, I realize that

161

you want me."

"Of course I do. That's never been an issue."

The city whipped past in a blur of pastel colors and ice beneath an arc of cloudless blue sky. Intent on finding distraction, I focused on the sights. Valentin rested his leg alongside mine and, thankfully, withdrew his hand. My erection soon subsided in the bitter cold. I set my longing aside, hoping that Valentin would deliver on the promise in his words and that I'd be ready to give in.

Chapter Fifteen

"So here we are." Valentin bounded up the front steps, the wood protesting beneath his feet.

An elderly couple, presumably Sergei and Anya, waited in the doorway, weeping openly while Yevgenny, the troika driver unloaded our luggage.

"It's so good to see you, young master." The man grasped Valentin's hand in both of his. "We've missed you so."

"You're too thin." The woman kissed Valentin's cheeks. "It's good that you're here, now I can make sure you eat properly.

Valentin stepped back. "Sergei, Anya, I'd like you to meet my very dear friend, Gabriel. He's going to be staying here. I'm hoping to persuade him to stay for a very long time. I'm hoping you'll help me, so you need to look after him as well as you look after me."

Sergei bowed briefly in my direction. "Welcome, sir. I hope you'll be happy here. We'll do our best to make you as comfortable as possible."

"I'm sure you will do splendidly, from all that Valentin has told me."

Anya's broad cheeks suddenly creased into dimples. She took my hand in hers. "We will look after you. Now both of you, come in. The house is nice and warm and I have *shchi* for you, because I know it is the young master's favorite."

Valentin kissed her cheek. "Anya, you never disappoint me. I have been longing for your *shchi*."

I followed him into the house, into a dark wood-paneled hall way. The warmth hit me as soon as I handed Anya my coat.

"Go into the sitting room, master. Sergei has a nice fire going in there, and there's tea and cakes for you both. I'll go and make sure Yevgenny puts your things in the right place." She hustled us forward, steering us into a long, bright room. Two chairs faced each other across a hearthrug beside the fire and, between them, a small table on which rested the promised tea and cakes.

Valentin sank into a chair and I took the other, holding my hands toward the fire.

"Paradise...at last." My companion settled back, stretching his legs across the rug. "How I have longed for this."

I took in the room, the gleaming wood paneling brightened by a few small paintings. The walls on either side of the fireplace were lined with shelves, all crammed with books — enough books to keep two people occupied for a very long time. A huge basket sat on the hearth, piled high with plenty of wood.

Valentin leaned forward and poured the tea. He raised his glass to mine. "Welcome, Gabriel. I hope you will be very happy here."

"Thank you. I hope so too." I sipped my drink and settled back into the embrace of the chair. I felt the house curl itself around me, offering comfort and refuge. I was hard pressed to remember the last time I'd felt so at peace.

* * * *

Valentin pushed his bowl away and leaned back in his chair. "So, what do you think of *shchi*?"

I wiped the last of the soup from my dish with a heel of bread. "Delicious." The combination of the journey, the comfortable house and the meal had conspired to make me drowsy. I took a mouthful of wine and glanced around the small dining room. The curtains were closed and a stove in the corner gave the room its warmth. "But now I'm ready to sleep."

"So am I. We can hibernate here. No footmen to wake us up. No need to present ourselves at the breakfast table. No need to dress for dinner."

"You're doing a very good job of persuading me that this is paradise on earth."

"That's because it is." He stood up and held out his hand. "We should sleep. It's been a long day."

I followed him up the narrow staircase. My room was across the hall from his. He paused beside the door and took my face between his hands. "Goodnight, Gabriel. Sleep well."

"I will."

He pressed his lips to mine — a sleepy, gentle kiss. "There's more where that came from. Remember that."

"Yes." I opened the door, reluctant to leave him. Knowing, that if I said the right words, I had no need to spend the night alone. Common sense, however, prevailed. As much as I wanted Valentin, I wanted him to court me. I wanted us to start from the beginning, I wanted to be sure that this was where I wanted to be for much longer than a winter. "Goodnight."

"Goodnight."

I slipped into my room. Someone, Anya presumably, had turned down the covers and laid my nightshirt across the bed. I washed with the water left for me on the dressing table, changed then crawled gratefully beneath the covers. I was already anticipating tomorrow, and what it might bring.

* * * *

Anya set breakfast on the table — bread, butter, cheese and a pile of blini. "It looks like you both arrived just in time."

I glanced past her to the window. The birch forest beyond was lost beneath a restless, shifting veil of white. Snow gathered in the corners of the window panes, softening the squares. "So it would seem."

165

Valentin reached for the butter and spread some lavishly on a piece of bread before helping himself to a piece of cheese. "Good, now we will be left in peace. It can snow as much as it likes."

I gazed at the snow. "I'm not used to seeing so much, especially after being in India for so long. The desert seems so far away."

"That's because it is. It's a lifetime away." Darkness clouded his features for the briefest of moments. "And that's where it needs to stay." He shuddered and gripped the butter knife until his knuckles whitened. "I wish I could bloody forget."

I reached across the table and covered his hand with mine. After a moment, the knife dropped to the table. "It will pass. Now that you are where you want to be, you can finally begin to heal properly."

"Do you really think so? There are times when I think that I'll never forget, that if I see a rat or a cockroach, I'll...I'll..." His breathing quickened, his eyes grew wide.

I rose and went to him, putting my arm around his shoulders. "Yes, I really think so. Those things can't hurt you anymore. You're home now. I'll look after you, Sergei and Anya will look after you."

Valentin rested his head on my shoulder. "Would you tell them? Tell Sergei and Anya what happened to me. I think they should know."

"Yes, I'll tell them, if that's what you want." I kissed the top of his head.

"It's what I want." He raised his head. "Thank you, Gabriel. Thank you for being here. I know what you've given up, what you've risked. I'll never be able to repay you."

I straightened up then returned to my side of the table. "I'm sure I'll think of something."

His smile was as sudden and brilliant as sunlight. "I'm sure you will."

We settled back down to breakfast while outside the snow

continued to fall, veiling the world in a shifting curtain of white.

* * * *

The sitting room was a haven of lamplit warmth against the rising blizzard. We sat in our respective chairs, both reading. Our legs stretched across the rug. The fire flickered in draughts from the wind, which also rattled the windows. The clatter of pots and aromas drifting from the direction of the kitchen promised another fine meal from Anya.

Sergei clomped into the room with another armload of wood. "It's getting bad out there now," he announced. "I thought it best to bring in as much wood as possible, so no one has to go out and get any."

Valentin lowered his book. "Excellent idea, Sergei. It's definitely not a good day for going anywhere. I take it we're all right for supplies?"

"Oh yes. The pantry is full and there's plenty of stuff in the shed too. We won't want for nothing." He strode back toward the door. "Anya says she's made a seed cake. She'll bring some with tea in a little while."

"Thank you. That would be very nice."

Sergei departed the room, closing the door behind him.

Valentin sighed. "We are lucky men, my friend. Here we are, nice and cozy in our hideaway, there's something good on the way for dinner, and we're about to have some of Anya's seed cake."

I peered over the top of my book. In the two days we'd been there, I could already see a difference in him. The dark circles were fading from beneath his eyes, the creases softening. He'd lost the gaunt pallor that had haunted him since leaving Bukhara. I realized, as I sat there admiring him, that I wanted him—not just to slake my desire, but because of who *he* was, what he had become to me. I crossed my legs and returned to my book, hoping that De Custine's *Empire of the Czar* might distract me.

"Are you all right?" Valentin set his book down on his lap.

"Never happier." It wasn't a lie. The weight and worry of the previous years had fallen away somewhere between St Petersburg and the *dacha*. "It can snow forever as far as I'm concerned. I'm content to stay here."

"I'm glad to hear you say that. Mind, the winters are long. You may feel differently by February."

"I've had years of relentless heat, I've been in Kabul in the winter, I've been places that I hope I never even hear of again, let alone visit. The idea of a nice, long winter when it snows so much that no one can possibly disturb us is my idea of heaven."

Valentin grinned. "Then, let's hope for a long, hard winter." He moved his legs so that one foot rested against mine.

I held my breath, astonished that even such a casual touch could distract me. Poor De Custine was losing his battle to keep my interest. I shucked my slipper and slowly eased my foot over his ankle.

"Gabriel…"

"Yes." I remained hidden behind my book.

"You are wicked. Very wicked."

"Nonsense."

"Here I am trying to come to grips with Herodotus and you appear to be intent on diverting my attention."

"It's very pleasant." I slid my foot along his calf, feeling the muscles tense beneath my touch.

"Yes…yes it is." He withdrew his leg and crossed it over the other, shifting in his chair. "Altogether too pleasant considering that Anya is likely to totter in here any moment now with tea and cake. I suggest we…pursue this…later."

"I would be amenable to that."

Somewhere in those few moments I realized that I had fallen in love with him. I realized that one winter would never be enough. I swallowed, gripped my book tightly and tried to read but my mind raced ahead. Would he make me leave in the spring? Would I find the words in me to tell him that I wanted to stay? I'd let him steer me to this place. I'd no sooner stepped off the *Russalka* that Valentin had undone the months I'd tried to forget him, leave him behind. I'd believed everything he'd told me and I hadn't the courage to ask him if he'd lied.

It was a relief when Anya bustled in a few minutes later with the afternoon tea. I let the simple pleasure of cake and tea chase away those niggling, stupid thoughts.

* * * *

Sergei had already added plenty of fuel to the stove, a fact for which I was grateful as the December wind slammed into the shuttered window. The house creaked with the sounds of its inhabitants settling down for the night— Sergei's rumbling cough as he secured the downstairs shutters, Anya setting out the breakfast things in readiness for morning and Valentin moving around his bedroom. I placed my clothes over the back of the chair and hesitated when I reached for my nightshirt, wondering if he would make good on his earlier suggestion. I decided to err on the side of pessimism and slipped it over my head before climbing beneath the covers, grateful for their weight and for the warming pan that Anya had placed in there earlier.

I extinguished the lamp and listened to the wind. Flames crackled happily in the stove, so loudly that I almost missed the snick of the door opening. Valentin's approach was heralded by a soft tread, the whisper of bare feet on a rug, his voice.

"Gabriel?"

I flung the covers back. The mattress dipped when he sat down. He fumbled for the matches on the bedside table. The brief sputtering was followed by the soft clink of glass and a flare of amber light. Valentin shrugged his way out of his nightshirt, letting it fall to the floor.

I removed mine and opened my arms.

He rolled on top of me, already erect. He moved his hips over mine with teasing slowness. "I had every intention of courting you, you know. But I decided that I couldn't wait, that the temptation of you being just across the hall was just too much."

"Perhaps I should ask you to leave and make you carry out your original promise." My member had stiffened and my senses reeled at the heat of Valentin's skin on mine.

"Perhaps, but I don't think you will. I think you're going to let me make love to you."

I held his face in my hands. "Is that what it is? Making love?"

He smiled, then silenced me with a kiss. It scorched its way through me, igniting my blood. I pushed my hips toward his.

"Ah, *Gavryushenka*." His whisper warmed my lips. "Of course it's making love. I passed the point of no return with you a very long time ago."

"How long ago?" I wound my fingers through his hair.

"The first time I kissed you." To demonstrate, he kissed me again—a long, slow kiss, as if he were savoring every moment.

"You've kept that quiet all this time?" My pulse fluttered, thoughts raced through my mind, memories, collecting those moments I missed.

"What purpose would it have served to say anything?" Valentin propped himself up on his elbows, his eyes suddenly serious. "What kind of fool would you have thought me if I'd told you? We were in a dangerous place. We needed our wits about us." He ducked his head and brushed his lips over my forehead. "Then events overtook us."

I stroked his cheek. "I never even…"

"Hush. It doesn't matter. We are both here, alive and healthy. We are out of danger, hidden away from the rest of the world with no one but ourselves to answer to. This seemed the right moment to tell you."

"Yes, it is." Contentment and something far deeper settled into my soul. Feelings I'd pushed aside for months rushed to the fore. "I suppose this is also the right moment to answer."

"And what is your answer?"

I curled my hand around the back of his neck. "What else could it be? Of course I love you. Would I have risked my neck to go the Emir if I didn't?"

Valentin smiled. "*Moi milyi.*"

"My soul," I repeated, drawing his head down until his brow rested on mine. "I like that."

"So you should, because you are." He closed his eyes and took a deep breath. "I have a question for you."

"Yes?"

"Will you stay?"

"Didn't I say I'd stay for the winter?" I didn't want to believe that he was asking me for more."

"Beyond that...beyond spring..." Valentin bit his lip.

I touched his cheek. "Just answer me this."

"What? Anything. You know that."

It was my turn to take a deep breath. "Kabul...were you telling the truth?"

His eyes darkened. He touched my lips with his for the briefest of moment. "Why do you think they sent me to Bukhara? You weren't the only one who was sent on a fool's errand, my love. Because I never talked, because I never did what my colleagues wanted me to do, I was sent to Bukhara as punishment."

"But the Adjutant General thinks the world of you."

"I'm sure he does, now that I've resigned. He can remember the good things that I did, not my failure. Does that put your mind at rest?"

"Yes." I finally let the past fall away. I consigned my friends and colleagues to their eternal rest.

"Then will you stay...forever?"

I didn't need to think, there was no need to hesitate. "Yes. I'll stay. Let's put the shadows and the game behind us. I'll stay forever."

"*Moi milyi*. Thank you." He shifted above me, stoking the fire.

My breath caught in my throat. I threaded my fingers through his hair and raised my hips once more to his, until our cocks were caught between us in an inferno of promise.

Valentin groaned and lowered his lips to my neck where he left a trail of heated little kisses. "Just think of the long, winter nights. We shall never be cold. I'll always keep you warm."

I tried to collect my thoughts, to reply, but all I could do was clasp his buttocks in an attempt to keep him close, so that nothing, not even air could pass between us. The scent of his arousal added to my desperation, fueling my desire. "Perhaps," I managed, "You could continue what you've started before I lose my mind with wanting you."

He laughed. His breath warm on my skin. "I love that I'm driving you mad." But he obliged, moving until his member rubbed against mine, creating a delicious friction.

I moved my hands along the smooth, warm sweep of his shoulders until he sat back on his heels.

"I want to be inside you."

"I want you there."

Valentin trailed his forefinger over the tip of my shaft, sweeping up the moisture that had gathered. Then he parted my legs with one hand before circling my entrance with his finger. I shivered at his touch, knowing what was to come. When he breached me I drew a deep breath and waited, trembling with the knowledge that he would soon be inside me. He withdrew, spat on his digit, then pushed it in once more, preparing me with great patience while I watched our flickering shadows on the wall. Snow whispered against the glass, driven by a rising wind. It didn't matter. I was where I wanted to be, with the man I wanted to be with. God willing, we had our whole lives before us.

"Are you ready, *gavryushenka*?"

"Always."

I took him in my arms and let him shut the rest of the world, and the past away.

Epilogue

"That's it then. Are you sure that's the right address?" I looked at the package in my hand, then at Valentin.

"It's the right address. Someone at the Ministry found it... somehow."

"All right." I turned and handed the parcel to the waiting boy. "To the post office with you and be quick about it." I pressed a coin into his hand.

The lad grinned and pocketed the coin. "Thank you sir, right away." He wheeled around and jogged along the snowy pavement, his breath rising like steam into the frosty air.

"That's it, then." Valentin threaded his gloved fingers through mine.

"That's it." I'd found the book when I'd been sorting through some things, searching for something else. The battered prayer book had fallen out of a bundle of clothes, neglected and forgotten for twenty years. I didn't want it — we'd managed to put Bukhara behind us. Valentin had written to a friend at the Ministry who'd discovered that Connelly's sister still lived. It seemed right to send it to her.

"Good." Valentin squeezed my hand. "Now it really is over."

"Yes it is."

We walked down the snowy street — a lifetime away from the shadows we'd left behind.

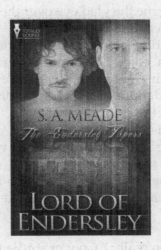

S. A. MEADE

The Endersley Papers

LORD OF ENDERSLEY

Lord of Endersley

Excerpt

Chapter One

Balls were meant to be held in the cooler months, in candlelit rooms in ancient mansions. We men weren't meant to be standing and perspiring in our finery, desperately seeking the faintest of breezes. I stared into my empty punch glass and wondered how soon I could decently leave. My cousin Harold had disappeared into another room in pursuit of a card game, leaving me with the cheerful suggestion to 'eye up the young ladies'.

As a visitor to this remote, godforsaken corner of India, it was more a case of the young ladies casting hopeful glances in my direction. New men were a talking point among the cantonment's matrons, anxious to marry their daughters off before the withering heat reduced them to wilted echoes of English roses. There was one now, Amelia-or-Emily

Winthrop, giving me the glad eye over the frantic fluttering of an ivory fan. I envied her the fan.

I hated to be rude. I glanced past her, caught by the glint of candlelight on gold. The women were fine enough in their silks and satins, but the soldiers were peacocks to their peahens, resplendent in their dress uniforms, trying not to look miserable in the stifling heat.

"Hellishly hot, isn't it?"

I turned at the sound of a familiar voice. "Ah, good evening, Cooper, yes it bloody is."

Septimus Cooper propped himself up against the wall, dabbing his scarlet face with a handkerchief. "Where's Fanning?"

"Cards."

"Stupid question really." Cooper studied his empty glass. "Left you to your own devices, did he?"

"He advised me to consider the ladies of the station."

He laughed. "Ever the attentive host."

"My cousin can be very attentive, but he can't resist the lure of the gaming tables. I'm grateful that he's been kind enough to look after a cousin he's never met before. He keeps a decent table and doesn't demand much in return, except for a bit of conversation. Once he realised I hadn't come here with the intention of seeking involvement in his business he was very accommodating indeed."

"He does look after his guests well...when he's not at the tables."

"There's not much else to keep a man entertained out here. I'll be glad to get back to England." I thought of Endersley in April, the cool wind blowing across the Downs, the slowly greening hedgerows and meadows alive with newborn lambs. Two more weeks and I would be on my way back there, in time for late summer, for long days and soft, cooling rain.

"I don't blame you, man. Things are getting devilishly uncomfortable here and I don't just mean the weather."

I watched Amelia-or-Emily Winthrop take to the dance

floor in the arms of an officer. He caught the eye more than she did with the gold braid of his dress uniform.

"Poor Billington." Cooper shook his head. "Nabbed by the predatory Miss Winthrop. I reckon you owe the good Captain a drink, Endersley. He's saved you from having to dance with her."

"He has indeed." I watched Billington, his back rigid as he led Amelia-or-Emily in the waltz. She smiled at him, fluttering her eyelashes at the same frantic speed that she'd fluttered her fan. Her dance card dangled from her wrist, no doubt waiting for my scribble. Billington never smiled, though a muscle twitched in his jaw. It shamed me that I found him more pleasing on the eye.

The waltz trailed to an end of jumbled notes and the rustle of skirts as couples parted or departed the dance floor. Amelia-or-Emily retreated to her mother and Billington headed in the opposite direction, towards us.

"Good evening, gentlemen." Billington wore the expression of a man who'd escaped a terrible fate.

"Captain."

Cooper glanced across the room. "Oh dear, the wife beckons. I'd better go and see what's irked her now." With a nod to us, he disappeared into the melee on the floor.

I spied Mrs Cooper, her lips pressed together, dark eyes glittering with disapproval, and felt more than a little sympathy for her husband.

"So, Endersley, I should think you'll be glad to be away from all of this." Billington leaned against the wall. The muscle still twitched in his cheek.

"I will. I was just thinking how much I'm looking forward to a rainy English summer."

Billington sighed. "I've been out here that bloody long I can't remember what summer rain feels like." His voice trailed away, and his eyes looked beyond the stifling confines of the large room.

We fell silent, me thinking of green grass and a sky full of familiar stars, Billington thinking of God knows what. I stole a glance at him and didn't envy him his uniform. Even his proximity to the window and the hidden *punkahwallah's* efforts couldn't erase the sheen of perspiration from his face.

"You'll do well to get out of here as soon as you can," he murmured, without prompting.

"I beg your pardon?"

"If you think it's hot now, in a few weeks' time it'll be unbearable. There's this hot wind that blows dust into every bloody crevice. It's miserable. You can't do anything much between sunrise and late afternoon."

"So I've heard. I'd planned on visiting Simla before heading down to Bombay."

"That's a very sensible notion." He glanced towards the veranda. "As is escaping this room before I suffocate. Are you coming?"

It sounded more like an order than a request. I followed Billington onto the veranda where several other gentlemen obviously shared the same idea. They greeted us with nods and carried on with their conversation. Billington leaned against the railing and stared out into the inky, airless dark. "I envy you escaping this place."

"It's not like you to be so blunt, sir." I'd met Billington at one of my cousin's parties not long after I'd arrived. We'd struck up an easy friendship united by our love of fine horses.

"There's more than the weather to worry about." He ran a careless hand through his hair. "There are rumours of trouble with the sepoys. This isn't going to be a safe place."

"I'd heard there could be trouble. So it's true?"

"It's more likely to happen than not." He turned around and stared back into the crowded party. "If I had my way I'd tell every civilian to get out but I'd be accused of scaremongering. If you can change your plans and leave sooner, then do it."

"Have you mentioned this to anyone else?"

"I've tried but I've been told that everything will be fine."

He looked at me, his eyes dark with a scarcely concealed fury. "I know my men. I know they're angry. God help us all if they mutiny."

The dark beyond the house was suddenly seething with unseen threats. Just when I'd become comfortable with the strangeness of the place, Billington reminded me that there was nothing easy or familiar about India. A peacock called out somewhere in the grounds—a haunting counterpoint to the echoes of laughter and music coming from beyond the open doors of the house.

"I consider you a friend." Billington folded his arms across his chest. "That's why I'm telling you this. Get out and get to Simla while you can."

"I'll do what I can." I tried to arrange everything in my mind, work out what needed to be done before I could leave. Even travelling in India was a logistical tangle.

"Excellent." He offered me a smile. "I always thought you were a man of good sense. What say we find ourselves a decent drink and do our best to avoid the attentions of the ladies."

"Sounds like an excellent notion."

He grinned then—a sudden, fierce warrior's grin. I pitied anyone who crossed him and wished God hadn't made me a man.

* * * *

The only time of day that the land was remotely hospitable was at first light. I rose early and went for an early morning ride to clear the fog of one drink too many. Thin shreds of mist lingered above the flat, drowsing land. The rising sun, swollen and red, spread a sullen light across the fields. The horse snorted when a bird hurried across the path and disappeared into a stand of bushes. I patted his neck and nudged him on. He snorted again and planted his feet, staring towards a stand of trees where several men squatted around a fire.

One of the men rose and walked towards me. "Good morning, *sahib*."

I was relieved his English was decent.

"Good morning."

"We have frightened your horse. I am sorry."

"It's all right."

The others remained beside the fire, casting glances towards us. I remembered Billington's words and didn't want to be there anymore.

"Would you like some help with your horse, *sahib*?"

"No, it's all right. I should be heading back anyway, before it gets too hot." It wasn't strictly a lie. The heat was rising with the sun. I wanted to be back on the veranda having *tiffin*.

He stepped back. "As you wish, *sahib*." He smiled again — a smile that didn't reach his eyes.

I turned the horse around and nudged it into a canter. It moved willingly enough, as anxious to return to the cantonment as I was.

Harold's shouts drifted across the yard. The *syce* took my horse, casting an uneasy glance at the house as he led the horse away.

"You stupid, clueless idiot! How many times have I told you that's not how to cook eggs? How many times have I told you I don't want your mucky curries ruining a perfectly good breakfast? You're bloody useless." The last insult was accompanied by the clatter of a pan or something similar hitting a hard surface. "I've half a mind to beat you until you get it right."

I hurried towards the house and ran across the veranda to the kitchen door. Harold, his face flushed, held a pan lid high and was advancing towards one of the servants, Samir, who was pressed to the wall, seemingly paralysed.

"What in God's name is going on here?" I burst into the kitchen, intent on stopping any brutality.

Harold spun around, pan lid still suspended in mid-air. "I was telling this useless idiot how not to make breakfast."

"With a pan lid?" I hated how unashamed he sounded. As if thrashing a servant for such a trivial oversight was something expected of him.

He lowered his arm. "I could always use my bare fists if you prefer."

"I see no need for brutality at all. The man made a simple mistake, there's no need to beat him for it."

"What I do with my servants is none of your business." His voice was cold.

"When you thrash a man for such a trivial offence, I intend to make it my business." I snatched the pan lid and tossed it through the open door. "If you want to beat someone, try me."

"You wouldn't." Harold stared at me, jaw slack.

"I bloody would." I stepped between him and Samir and rolled up my shirtsleeves. "It's not that I don't appreciate your generous hospitality, cousin, but if that hospitality comes at the expense of a man's well-being, then I'd rather just pack my things and go."

"For Christ's sake, Jacob, don't you think you're overreacting a bit here?" Harold held his hands out, palms up, half a smile on his face. "If it makes you happy, I'll humour you. There's no need to take on and talk of leaving."

I glanced at Samir who still clung to the wall. "It's all right. He won't hurt you now. It might be a good idea if you were to remake his breakfast."

He nodded, all wide-eyed and silent.

"Without the local embellishments, please."

"Yes, *sahib*." He hurried back to his station.

I looked at Harold. "Now, why don't we go and sit on the veranda and enjoy what's left of the cool morning. You can have a sherry to calm your temper." I took him by the arm and marched him out of the kitchen.

"How bloody dare you," he growled.

"Oh shut up, Harold. It bloody serves you right for drinking rum for breakfast."

His breath reeked of it. He glared at me with angry, bloodshot eyes. "Don't lecture me on my drinking habits, cousin."

I shoved him onto the veranda and pushed him into a chair. "I don't care if you think I've overstepped the mark by telling you off in front of your own servants. While I'm here, and while I hold the strings to your purse, you will not abuse your staff, do you understand me?"

"By God, you can be an arrogant bastard sometimes, Jacob."

"Do you want this money or don't you?"

Harold's cheeks flushed—plum clashing awkwardly with his gingery side whiskers. He swallowed and wiped his mouth with the back of his hand. "You know I need it."

"Then I suggest you refrain from treating your servants like slaves." I sank into the other chair, still shaking with anger.

Harold reached for the sherry with a shaking hand but said not another word until *tiffin* arrived.

"I'm going upcountry for a few days." Harold sipped his tea. "You'll be all right, won't you? The servants will take good care of you."

"I'll be fine." I welcomed the chance of some solitude. "I need to start thinking of making a move myself. I was talking to Marcus Billington last night and he suggests that I head for Simla sooner rather than later."

Harold sighed. "Let me guess, he was whining about the sepoys again, preaching doom and gloom."

"I wouldn't say he was whining. He seemed quite certain."

Harold's cup hit the saucer with a rattle. "He's a scaremonger. He's always looking for trouble where there isn't any. You'll be safe enough here."

I kept drinking my tea. "If you say so."

"I've known Billington for a few years. He's a good man but he can be a bit overcautious. Damn fine horseman, mind."

"Yes, he is."

Amongst other things.

* * * *

Noshad, the *syce*, led my horse out with a grin. "Here you are, *sahib*. I hope you and the Captain enjoy your ride. It is sensible to ride with someone now."

"Thank you." I smiled back.

Noshad's smile disappeared. He stroked the horse's nose. "You must be very careful."

I climbed into the saddle. "I will. I don't intend to ride without company."

"Good." He stepped back as Marcus rode into the yard on his bay.

"Good morning." He reined his horse in beside mine. "Are you ready?"

I checked the girth, found it tight and nodded. "Let's go before it gets too hot."

We trotted out of the yard and headed towards the fields. The horses pinned their ears back and bared their teeth, posturing and jogging, impatient for a gallop. I sat deep in the saddle and kept my hands still. Billington rode in silence, his eyes on the flat, parched land lying in wait for the monsoon. The breeze ruffled his hair. I tightened my fingers around the reins and thought it best to concentrate on keeping my horse in hand.

"Race you," he said.

"To the trees?"

"Yes. Loser has to provide dinner." He grinned, threw his hands forward and spurred his horse. It squealed and plunged into action. Mine threw in a spirited buck and leapt after the bay. I leaned low in the saddle and urged the horse on, anxious to ride out of the cloud of chalky dust Marcus' horse left in its wake.

I had plenty of horse beneath me, I gave it a bit more rein and it sprang forward, drawing level with the bay.

Marcus turned and laughed. "The race isn't won yet, my

friend." He kicked the bay's flanks. It pinned its ears back and quickened.

My horse fought valiantly to keep pace, but the reins soon slackened as we sped towards the line of trees at the end of the track. Marcus still had plenty of horse in hand and I was left with a face full of dust. I eased my horse up and cantered a length or two behind to where Marcus waited in the grey dappled shade of the trees.

"That was a very poor performance, Mr Endersley."

"I was looking after the animal's legs. The ground's hard."

"Now I get a splendid dinner at your cousin's table."

"Without my cousin. He's upcountry for a few days."

"Even better. I can save myself some money since he won't be there to fleece me at cards."

"I'll make sure to tell the kitchen staff to excel themselves."

"I'm sure they will." He took a flask from his saddlebag and drank deeply. "Water?" He held the flask out.

"Thanks. Inhaling all your damn dust has made me thirsty."

He laughed. "That'll teach you to be cautious."

The water was warm and slightly brackish. I took a few sips and handed the flask back.

Billington tucked the flask back into the saddlebag and gathered up his horse's reins. "I suppose we'd better head back before the heat gets the better of us."

We turned our tired horses around and walked them sedately along the track. The heat was rising with the sun, blanketing the silent landscape with shimmering mirages. My companion was silent again, watchful, his eyes narrowed. I tried to occupy my mind with what to request for dinner but my gaze drifted to Billington, noting the ease with which he rode — one hand on his hip, his long thighs at a comfortable angle, their shape revealed by his breeches. I almost asked for the flask again, to pour water over my head in an attempt to change the unwholesome direction in which my mind was heading.

It was almost a relief to reach the cantonment. We parted

at the gate.

"I'll be there for eight." Marcus shifted in the saddle. "To collect my winnings."

More books from S.A. Meade

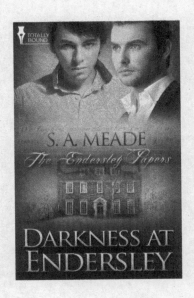

Joshua thought he'd left his past behind, but there's something in the darkness at Endersley.

He's not ready for the turbulence caused by the new 'lord of the manor'.

Michael and Paul fight to survive in a land frozen by endless winter.

The horror of Evan and Colin's stolen summer may be over but the nightmares remain.

About the Author

S.A. Meade

S.A. Meade has recently returned to England after 8 years in Arizona, where she learned to love air conditioners and realised that rain wasn't such a bad thing after all. She lives with her husband, son and two cats in one of the most beautiful villages in Wiltshire and is partial to gin and tonic with loads of ice and lemon.

S.A. Meade loves to hear from readers. You can find contact information, website details and an author profile page at https://www.pride-publishing.com/